SOLSTICE WITCH

A SEASHELL COVE PARANORMAL COZY
MYSTERY
BOOK 6

T. THORN COYLE

AUTHOR'S NOTE

One character had a name change. Ah Lam Wu was originally Angelica Wu in my head, but as there was already an Angie in the series, her name changed to Ah Lam Wu in Tarot Witch—the book in which she first appears. The name was mistakenly reverted to Angelica in subsequent novels. Those novels will be retroactively corrected, reinstating her correct name.

1

It was four in the afternoon, and dusk was settling over Seashell Cove. Given the dark clouds massed over the sleepy town, there would be no sunset kissing the gray churn of waves today.

Rhiannon snored softly in the front display window, curled up next to a stack of Christmas ghost romances. Her furry black side rose and fell, and her front paws twitched. I would say my cat was hunting mice in her dreams, except Rhiannon never hunted anything other than treats.

And criminals.

She would also balk at being called "my" cat. Rhiannon is definitely her own person. As a matter of fact, she'll most likely tell you she's my boss, not the other way around.

The gargoyles, Petal and Posey, dozed on top of two bookcases. They'd become pretty good alarm systems for the shop, but when nothing was happening? Turns out sentient stone sculptures like to nap almost as much as cats.

Staring out at Main Street and the bright twinkle lights, listening to some classic Loreena McKennitt, I sighed. Now that the shop was finally in the black, it was good to have a breather in the midst of the holiday rush. My handsome geek of a boyfriend was cooking me dinner later, and promised me a neck rub, too.

I should have felt content. Right? No one had left a dead rat on my doorstep. No one had died. Nothing had been stolen, not even the small tchotchkes we keep around for holiday impulse buyers.

But no. I wasn't content. I was restless.

It felt as if I needed to look over my shoulder for what was coming. Or as if the other rain boot was about to drop.

Sighing again, I wandered between the long rows of bookcases that marched down the center of the store, straightening spines and reshelving books led astray by customers from the lunchtime rush.

Opening my witch's senses, I scanned the shop I'd inherited from my father—The Widening Gyre—trying to get a feel for what troubled me.

Nothing. Like, literally nothing.

Even Biff the ghost was quiet. He hadn't thrown a book in days, only popping out to startle and delight a few customers who were looking for gifts before Yule, but were happy to also take selfies in the haunted store.

Cyrus, my honorary magical uncle, was off who knows where, though he'd promised he and his new girl-friend, Ah Lam Wu, would be back before Solstice Eve.

"Silly," I said to myself, after moving *The Devil's Dictionary* from the occult section and back where it belonged —in language reference—for the tenth time in as many weeks. "That's what's wrong."

This was the time of year I missed my parents most. It was easy to forget when the shop was full, my manager, Duncan, was frantic, and the teens who helped out part time were at the wrapping station set up on one end of the front counter.

But when things grew quiet like this? And I was all alone with no one but a sleeping cat and two dozing gargoyles for company?

Well.

"Hope you and Mom are okay, Dad." I whispered to the history section. History was his favorite topic. He would sit in front of the fire at home, cup of tea close to hand, and read for hours.

"I'm finally settling into this whole Justice business. I think I'm even getting good at it. Of course, I have a lot of help, just the way you and Mom must have."

I had fought against being magical Justice of our area at first. It took me several months to really step into the role. As a matter of fact, some people even accused me of being whiny.

Most of those people were Rhiannon, my mouthy cat. But she has opinions about everything.

The bells hanging from the front door clanged, announcing the arrival of a customer.

I walked to the front, to be greeted by the sight of a large white man in a red coat, with a sprig of holly pinned to his lapel. He had short brown hair and a neatly trimmed brown beard topped with rosy cheeks and sparkling brown eyes.

"Hello!" I said. "Welcome to The Widening Gyre. Is there something I can help you find?"

His smile was arresting, broad and bright, beaming like the winter sun. Not that we saw much of the winter sun on the Oregon Coast in December.

Also, I swear his eyes twinkled. If it weren't for the brown hair, I'd say the guy bore an uncanny resemblance to Old Saint Nick. Not the red-suited guy made famous by the Coca Cola company, but the older, European version.

"I'm shopping for gifts," he said. "And books make the best gifts, don't they?"

"I wouldn't be a bookseller if I didn't agree." I smiled back, my melancholy brooding gone. "If there's anything in particular that I can help you find, please let me know. Otherwise, enjoy!"

"Oh. I intend to," he said, wandering down the side aisle toward the Science Fiction and Fantasy sections.

After he disappeared, I wondered what brought him to our little burg this time of year. I would certainly remember having seen him if he lived anywhere within ten miles of Seashell Cove. There just weren't that many bookshops in the area, and he kind of stood out.

I puttered some more, rearranging the front window displays until Rhiannon swiped at me. The cat loved her window display bed, and her naps. Luckily, the customers love her, too.

That done, I headed toward the tiny kitchen off the main room of the store and put on the kettle for tea. It was too late for my favorite English Breakfast, but a nice comforting cup of mint would do.

Before the kettle could boil, the bells sounded again. Drat. Did that mean Mr. Red Winter Coat had left before buying anything?

If I was lucky, it meant another customer had arrived.

With a longing look at the kettle, I headed back toward the front. The gargoyles stirred above me, high on their bookshelf perches.

That meant someone new had arrived. But when I got to the clear space between the front door and the checkout counter, nothing was there.

::*Look down,*:: Rhiannon said inside my head. She sat perched on the edge of the front display, books and Solstice lights behind her. Her green eyes stared down at a spot around my knees.

I looked down, and staring up at me with red-rimmed, dark brown eyes, was an elf with skin the same pale green as Elphaba from *Wicked*.

And by elf I don't mean the tall Sidhe types that figure so largely in fantasy novels. No. This was an honest-to-Goddess, red-pointy-hat-and-striped-stockings elf. Like the kind you think of in Santa's workshop.

Or those ones that make cookies they sell in most major US supermarkets. Except for the green skin and all.

The little elf said nothing. Just sniffed, then wiped a button nose on a long red sleeve.

"Are you okay?" I asked. "Can I help you?"

"He is coming!" the elf squeaked out, then clapped a hand to its tiny rosebud mouth as if surprised.

"He's coming?" I asked. "Who? Who is coming?"

"I don't knoooowwww," it wailed, sniffles turning into outright sobbing. "I don't know where I am. I don't know who I am!"

It hunched over itself, little arms wrapped around its chubby torso, eyes squinched shut.

Great. What was I supposed to do about an elf with amnesia? Was it some sort of messenger? Or were those first words just nonsense?

With a soft thump, Rhiannon leapt from the display window and padded softly toward the elf, bumping it with a black shoulder.

The elf's sobs slowed. It cracked open one brown eye.

"N-nice kitty?"

Rhiannon bumped it again and started purring.

This was some sort of Solstice miracle. Rhiannon mistrusts all new people, and it takes a lot to make her purr. Like, a lot a lot.

Did I mention she's a bit cranky?

Overhead, I heard the gargoyles shift and creak, moving closer to watch the action.

I crouched down, tugging at my jeans, which were getting a little tighter than I liked, though Stefon wouldn't complain. He likes tight jeans. But holiday season is that way. I don't have time to go jogging while it's light out, and running on an Oregon Coast beach in the dark is a recipe for certain death.

"Do you remember anything?" I asked. Rhiannon bumped my knee, and I gave her head a scratch. The rumbling purr continued. Rhiannon really liked this little elf. Maybe her friendship with Preston the gnome had softened her heart toward small people with pointy hats or something.

The elf lifted one booted foot, then the other, jingling softly with every movement.

"No." It sniffed. The tears were drying up at least, thank Hecate, Diana, and Mother Night. "All I remember is the sound of bells. And that I was supposed to tell you he is coming."

I nodded in what I hoped was an encouraging fashion.

"That's good. Do you know what brought you in here?"

The elf looked around the store, as if seeing it for the first time. The poor thing was really out of it.

"I..." It looked at me with those big brown eyes again. "I'm not sure. I think there was a sparkle outside. And when I opened the door, it felt good in here."

A sparkle outside? I glanced at Rhiannon, who flicked an ear, but said nothing.

"That's the Solstice Sprite." Petal's gravelly voice sounded from just above my head.

"Solstice Sprite?" I looked up at the stone face staring down at me. Petal's bow was on the left side of her head today, set at a fetching angle.

"The sparkle thingy. Outside. It's been hanging around after dusk for the past week. We thought you knew." That was Posey. The one without the bow. If the gargoyles ever decided to change their sartorial decorations, I would be in a pickle. That bow was my main way of telling the two apart.

That's laziness on my part, I know. The gargoyles do

have different facial features and slightly different builds. So what if their skin is a uniform shade of gray? That doesn't mean they actually look the same.

"Wait here," I said to the little elf. "Rhiannon will take care of you. I'll just be a minute."

With a clang of bells, I opened the door and walked out into the dark, frigid evening.

2

"Hello?" I asked the night air. "Anyone there?"

The tang of cold salt air and the distant rush and tumble of waves at the bottom of the cliffs answered me. Main Street was fairly quiet, with just a few people heading to dinner at Vargas's Tamales next door and some stragglers heading into festively lit shops for gifts and supplies.

Down the street, someone barked out a laugh, and music exited the door of the newly opened bar—the Troll's Lair—five doors down. The raucous noise was just as quickly hushed when the door closed. Some locals had complained when the bar opened, figuring it would bring a "bad element" to our sleepy downtown. I rolled my eyes at the curmudgeons. Seashell Cove needed more places for people to hang out, in my opinion. And there was nothing wrong with folks wanting to get together for a beer after work sometimes.

Wishing I'd thrown on a jacket, I took a breath of the cold, salty air and centered myself. Black boots planted firmly on the sidewalk, I reached out again with my extra senses, scanning the area.

There. To my left, just at the corner of the shop where the planter boxes marked off the beginning of our tiny parking lot, was a shimmer. Walking slowly and carefully, I reached the corner just in time to see a sparkly flash of lights slowly rise and turn, before they sped off toward the ocean, into the winter-dark sky.

"Dang," I said, staring toward the direction the lights had gone. "Missed it."

When I turned, Rhiannon blinked at me from inside the big display windows. She stood next to a book we'd just gotten in, a collection of magical short stories called *A Procession of Faeries*. Did it mean something, or was it just coincidence? Sometimes it was hard to tell.

You'd think being a hereditary witch and a Justice, I would know when something was a message versus when it was a random, ordinary occurrence. But here's the secret about magic: there are times when it hits you over the head like a two-ton sparkly wand, and other times when it is subtle as an ocean mist. Young witches learn to distinguish between those two, because they're looking for them. But the third thing about magic that witches need to learn is this: Sometimes a book is just a book. Sometimes a song is just a song. Sometimes that ache in your hand is just from too much time spent on the computer or playing racquetball.

Not everything the cosmos sends your way is a coded message only you can figure out.

But sixty percent of the time? It is.

"Discernment is the witch's most important tool," my

mother used to say. And the older I got, the more I realized that was true. Sure, the world is filled with more magic than most people realize, but sometimes a witch needs to deal with the stuff of ordinary life. Like health care and balancing her account sheet. Or still fitting into her size sixteen jeans by the time February rolls around.

With one last look around, I headed back toward the door of The Widening Gyre. A breeze swept through the parking lot, causing me to shiver. It rattled through the green holly bushes in the planter boxes, where a soft tinkle reached my ears.

Bending down toward the glossy green, spiny leaves, I peered past a red cluster of berries and saw a small silver bell. My fingers stroked the smooth, cold surface, and the bell spoke to me.

::I am home,:: it whispered in my psychic ears. *::I am home.::*

Okay then. If the bell thought it was home, who was I to argue? I plucked it from the bush, pricking my fingers on the spine of one green leaf. Blood beaded on my fingertip, threatening to drop onto the plant.

"Oh, no you don't!" I said, sticking my finger in my mouth to swipe away the dot of blood. No way was I giving a holly plant a blood offering, no matter how small. Not until I figured out what this bell was doing here, and what the plant wanted, other than a drop of my witchy essence.

Dropping the bell in my pocket, I reached for the door. I was well and truly cold now, and wanted nothing more than to brew that cup of tea and get the shop ready for tomorrow.

Unfortunately, there was an amnesiac elf to deal with, strange fairy lights to investigate, and who knew what else was coming on the winter winds?

And where had the man with the holly sprig on his red coat gone? Had he left when the elf arrived?

No wonder I'd felt unsettled. My subconscious was telling me to be on my guard. Well, I certainly was now. There was no escaping it.

A car door shut behind me.

"Babe?"

I turned to see my big mountain of a knight striding toward me in boots and jeans, a jacket over his standard hoodie the only concession to the December weather.

The tension coiled in my belly relaxed, just seeing the smile playing beneath his dark curly beard, lighting up his deep brown eyes, which were just a few shades darker than his lush skin. A powerful mountain of a man, Stefon is the only person who can make large, athletic me feel the slightest bit delicate.

I folded myself into his open arms and sighed, smelling the Stefon scent of him. No matter what, he always smelled like home.

"Why are you out here?" he asked. "And where's your jacket?"

"I was only supposed to be out here for a minute." I looked up into his handsome face. My literal knight in shining armor, Stefon is not only an in-demand game coder and sci-fi geek, but also a red-belted Knight in the Society for Medieval Anachronism, or the SMA. I gave his lips a soft kiss before pulling away.

"I'll tell you about it inside," I said. "But I warn you, there's an elf in there, and it seems lost."

"An elf? Like from Lord of the Rings?"

I shook my head. "No. An elf, like from Santa's workshop."

He gave a soft laugh and muttered something that sounded a lot like "I never expected my life to be this way," before opening the door and letting us in to light and warmth and the smell of hot chocolate.

                                3

The little elf sat on the floor, leaning up against the counter, a small mug of what was definitely hot chocolate spiced with cinnamon in its pale green hands. Rhiannon sat next to him, with Petal and Posey crouched on the counter just above the pair.

The gargoyles looked very pleased with themselves, though Posey had a telltale dusting of brown powder on his paws. Or claws. Or feet. Or whatever we're supposed to call gargoyle appendages.

"Hot chocolate?" I asked the room. "How in the world is there hot chocolate?"

"We made it!" Petal said proudly. "Posey learned how to use the kettle so we could have tea when the shop is closed, and I learned how to open cupboards! It seemed like the little guy here needed some cheering up."

I groaned inside, not wanting to think of the disaster waiting for me in the kitchenette, but I had to admit that the elf did look better.

"Did the elf say anything?" I asked Rhiannon.

::*Nothing useful,*:: she replied inside my head.

I crouched down again and peered at the sad green face. "Are you feeling better?"

It offered up a shy smile that was here and gone in a blink. "I like the chocolate. And everyone here is very nice."

Then a cloud passed over the pointy little face. "But I don't remember who I am. Or why I'm here."

Digging into my pocket, which is no small feat with jeans this tight, let me tell you, I pulled out the silver bell.

"Do you recognize this?"

The elf frowned, then shook its feet, setting the bells on the little boots to ringing.

We all examined its ankles, but the bells there were a brassy gold, not silver.

The elf looked at me, shaking its head sadly. "I thought I did, but maybe I don't."

"That's okay," I said. "Just take your time. We'll figure it out. Meanwhile, did any of you see where the tall man in the red coat went?"

Posey and Petal both slowly shook their heads with a slight grinding sound that still made me wince. Sentient stone doesn't move very fast. And isn't super stealthy.

Well, that was another mystery. Did Mr. Red Winter Coat have anything to do with the bell in my pocket? Or was it left by the Solstice Sprite?

The shop door opened with a bang and a clatter and in burst Tracy and Tabitha, my two teenage assistants. Best friends, they are opposites. Tracy, another hereditary witch, is white, blond, and bubbly, and prone to wearing jeans and pastel shirts. Tabitha is Asian-American, a

Wiccan, and as Goth as I used to be in my Portland college days.

Both wore the standard Pacific Northwest anoraks over jeans. Tabitha's was black, with a fake-fur-edged hood, while Tracy's jacket was burgundy.

Tabitha's dark hair with its purple streak framed her cheekbones in a wedge poking from beneath the black watch cap with a pink pentagram on the front. Tracy's blond hair straggled from beneath her own cap, which was powder blue.

"Rhiannon told us there was an elf!" Tracy said, practically bouncing in her boots. "Mom dropped us off right away! She's parking the car, but we couldn't wait!"

Carol appeared at the door right as her daughter spoke the words. It was almost as if Tracy had conjured her into existence. Carol was taller than Tracy, with the same blond hair and long legs. She's much thinner than I am, but just as strong, and a powerful witch in her own right. Carol had taken on Tabitha as an honorary daughter, since Tabitha's own parents were vampires and couldn't always make it out to school events, and certainly couldn't drive her to soccer practice or magic lessons.

Both teens took the lone Seashell Cove bus when they could, but service was spotty out here on the coast.

I was glad to have all three of them on my side. But that begged the question.

"Rhiannon can broadcast messages now?" I asked no one in particular.

I looked down at the black cat who had suddenly decided her right paw needed a good wash.

"Rhiannon? Have you been practicing psychic communication behind my back?"

I wasn't angry, but I did feel a bit hurt. After all, she was supposed to be my familiar, but here she was keeping secrets from me and talking to the teens? It was only recently she'd finally 'fessed up that she could use mind speech at all, and I assumed it required physical proximity.

She looked up and blinked. ::*I wanted to surprise you, but needed to test some things out first.*::

"Babe," Stefon squeezed my arm in reassurance. He can always tell when I'm upset.

I exhaled a noisy breath. "That makes sense, I guess. But tell me next time, okay? We can work on this stuff together."

And should be working on it, actually. Uncle Cyrus said I needed to strengthen my bond with Rhiannon if I was going to level up in my Justice work.

That's the other thing about magic they never tell you: as soon as you start to feel comfortable in your skin, and like your life and skills have stabilized, the universe, or the Powers—or whatever you want to call them— decide you need to work harder.

And do more. Always more.

"Hey little guy." Tracy crooned at the elf, who looked up at the teen with saucer eyes. "My name is Tracy."

The elf's brown eyes teared up again. "I'm sorry, but I don't know my name."

"That's okay, little dude," Tabitha chimed in. "We'll figure it out."

She looked around. "Won't we?"

"We made hot chocolate!" Posey said. "It helped!"

Wait a minute. I'd been calling the elf "it" but everyone else seemed to think it was male.

"Hey," I crouched down. "I know you don't remember much, but do you know your gender?"

The elf tilted its little green head. "I think I'm a he. At least, that's what I feel like."

Okay. That was one thing settled at least.

::I think I found something while you were outside,:: Rhiannon interrupted my thoughts.

"What's she saying?" Stefon asked. He can't hear mind speech but has learned to read the signs and can tell when it's happening now, kind of like he can tell when a ghost is in the room, even if he can't see or hear them.

"Rhiannon thinks she found something," I translated. "What is it?"

She pawed at the back of the little elf's red tunic. The elf reached back to scratch his neck.

"Tracy?" I asked.

The teen reached out and grabbed the back of the elf's collar, turning it inside out.

"Oh! There's a tag!"

"What does it say?" Carol asked. The tall witch had unzipped her jacket and looked ready for action; hands loose at her sides in case a sudden burst of magic was called for.

Tracy peered at the pale little square of cloth.

"Polar Projects," she read. "Spells made. Wishes granted. Good will spread."

Tracy's blue eyes were wide, darting between me, her mother, and her best friend. "Does this mean...?"

"Are you from the North Pole?" Stefon asked.

The little elf burst into sobs again, cradling his head in his tiny green hands, hot chocolate long forgotten.

"I don't know!" he wailed. "But I want to go hooomme!"

As I stared down at the sorrowful creature, I realized everyone was looking at me again. Expecting me to have the answers.

But as usual, I didn't have the answers. But I knew how to get them.

"Okay," I said, hands on my curvy hips. "Tracy. Tabitha. You research elf sightings and Santa's workshop and anything else you can think of. Carol? You text Delta and Preston. The gnome might know something. Petal and Posey, it's your job to keep the elf protected, okay?"

Both gargoyles nodded in agreement.

"What about me?" Stefon asked.

"You think of any gaming lore that has the slightest thing to do with Solstice, elves, the North Pole...anything at all."

One thing I'd learned as Stefon's girlfriend is that gamer geeks—whether the tabletop variety or the video kind—love to hide real information and folklore inside game tech of all kinds. Clues about other realms are everywhere if you just know where and how to look.

Then I looked at my cat. "Rhiannon? You and I are going to consult Mom's crystal ball."

I just hoped my dead mother's spirit had some intel to share. Because once again we were on a case where I hadn't a clue.

4

Stefon was in the living room of the Craftsman cottage that was my childhood home, laying a fire in the hearth. My father had lived alone in the hundred-plus-year-old house after my mother died. Now that my father was dead, too, the place was mine, all mine.

Though she was a shop cat, Rhiannon loved the cottage during winter, and came home with me far more often in the dark months, wanting to cozy up next to the fire.

::*Could you hurry up?*:: she said, staring at me from the queen size carved wood bed. She lay smack in the middle of the big green Celtic knot comforter, looking like a cat from the Book of Kells.

"Look, cat, I know you want to go sit by the fire, but I need your help here."

That wasn't strictly true, and I could tell Rhiannon knew it. I would need her help once Mom's crystal ball was set up and the scrying began, but right now? Frankly,

I just wanted the company. Something about the lost elf still wasn't sitting right with me.

"Did you notice anything else about the shimmering lights outside the shop? Was it the Solstice Sprite?"

If such a thing existed, though, why not?

I could practically feel the wheels in Rhiannon's hard little head turning as I gathered an altar cloth, some candles, and my favorite incense, and set them on my dresser next to the wooden box containing my mother's scrying ball.

::I don't think it was a sprite. Could you get an energy signature while you were outside?::

I shook my head. "No. I just saw some lights rise into the air and speed off toward the ocean cliffs."

Which was strange. I should have been able to sense what the heck the thing was. "Do you think it's connected to our elf friend?"

Rhiannon didn't bother to reply. Cats don't repeat the obvious. That only seems to be something humans do. Well, other people probably did, too. Like my friend Tetris's golden lab.

Oh. That's another thing about witches. We call a lot of things *people* that other humans don't. That's because there are more sentient beings walking and flying in the world than most humans ever notice, let alone comprehend. So yeah, dogs and cats and gargoyles and gnomes? All people. Rocks and trees? Most of them are people, too.

"Okay. I have everything. Let's go."

Rhiannon leapt from the bed and padded down the hallway. I followed, juggling my magical objects in both arms. The scent of woodsmoke and the crackle of the fire greeted us as we entered the living room. Stefon sat on the comfy sofa, stocking feet propped on the long wood coffee table, staring into the flames. The two overstuffed chairs facing the coffee table were empty, of course, though sometimes I swore a sliver of my father's essence occupied his favorite old wood and leather reading chair.

Stefon reached out to take some of the things from me, holding them in his broad lap as I flicked open the blue velvet altar cloth and spread it across the coffee table.

"Thanks for lighting the fire. It smells nice."

It felt nice, too. I really had gotten chilled standing outside the shop earlier.

"I love my gas fire," he said, "but there's nothing like burning real wood. Reminds me of camping out."

Stefon had been trying to convince me to go to another SMA camping event, but I'd been too busy trying to get The Widening Gyre back on track. I enjoyed the medieval camping events a lot. There was something about being in a beautiful location, surrounded by nature and a sea of canvas tents with pennants waving, and folks dressed in fantastic costumes, er, *garb*, walking by. Plus, they always had cool traditional crafting classes.

Not that I have time for any hobbies.

"Maybe we can go to an event this spring or summer," I said. "Now that Tracy and Tabitha are trained in more of the shop operations, they can back Duncan up so I can go out of town."

Two years ago, I never thought I'd say those words. Any small business owner will tell you how hard it is to take time off. Ever. But my dad used to remind me that life was more important than the bookshop, and that my first responsibilities were to the magical community, and myself.

The fire at my back, I set up the small altar. Crystal ball in the center, on its tiny circular stand, a beeswax taper flanking each side.

I shook some loose incense into the stone holder, piled it into a shallow cone, and lit a piece of kindling from the fire. Fragrant smoke rose in the air. I cupped my hands over it, wafting some of the incense smoke over my head as Rhiannon and Stefon watched.

Picking up the crystal ball, I passed the orb through the smoke, cleansing it, getting it ready for what I hoped were the visions to come.

"You weren't going to call me?" My uncle's voice came from the kitchen door. I stifled a curse, the crystal orb almost slipping from my hands.

"Dang it, Cyrus! You never give a witch any warning!"

I carefully placed Mom's crystal back on its holder as my dapper uncle glided into the cozy living room. He was dressed in dark wool slacks, some kind of Italian leather shoes that cost more than the shop lease, and a long navy wool coat over a burgundy sweater.

Firelight danced across the dark bald dome of his head and his eyes looked serious.

"You, my Goddess Niece, are supposed to tell me when things are afoot."

"Afoot?" I asked, as Rhiannon wound her furry black body around Cyrus's legs in greeting. Traitor. "What are we, in a Sherlock Holmes novel?"

Stefon stifled a laugh as Cyrus glared down at me.

"A lost elf shows up at your bookshop and you don't even think to ping me? Not a text, not a psychic shout?"

"Oh, sit down," I huffed. "You and Ah Lam Wu were off who knows where, and I'm supposed to keep you apprised of every little thing that happens here? Maybe when you start telling me where you are and what you're working on, I'll return the favor."

I wasn't usually so snippy with my warlock of an honorary uncle, but I'd been on edge all day and the feeling had only increased with the arrival of the little elf.

Cyrus *humphed*, but said nothing, just removing his coat, tossing it over the arm of the sofa, and sliding into a waiting chair.

"Tell me what happened," he said. "But first, do you have any wine?"

Typical. A warlock shows up unannounced and wants refreshments.

"Nothing you'd find drinkable," I said, which was true. I was a screw top or box wine kind of witch, while Cyrus was strictly high end. He had ten times my income —at least—and the taste to match. I was never sure where exactly his money came from, just that he'd always seemed to have it. At least for as long as he'd been in my life, which was from birth. My birth. Not his.

He frowned, then disappeared.

"Holy crap!" Stefon shouted, leaping to his feet.

My own heart raced as I stared at the empty chair my uncle had occupied mere seconds ago. Rhiannon was the only one who looked unperturbed, curled up on a little rug next to the hearth, half dozing.

::You know he does that, right? That all warlocks pop in and out at will?::

I narrowed my eyes at her. "Of course, I know 'he does that.' But he always enters from another room. He never pops in and out in front of people."

At least not that I knew. Maybe warlocks on the Witches and Warlock's Super Secret Society—my name for them, not theirs—did it all the time.

Stefon still stood, panting, head whipping around the room, poised to strike. What he thought he was going to fight, I wasn't sure.

Then, just as suddenly as he had popped out, Uncle Cyrus popped back in, again seated in Dad's reading chair, but this time holding one of those fancy broad-bottomed wine glasses, filled halfway with a red wine that gleamed like a ruby in the firelight.

Stefon's right hand flew to his chest, and he sat down, hard, on the sofa.

I looked at my uncle and rolled my eyes.

"Neat trick. Are you happy you almost scared my boyfriend to death?"

Cyrus just raised an eyebrow at me and took a slow sip of wine, then turned to give Stefon an appraising look.

"He'll live. Stefon is nothing if not strong. It's part of why he's a suitable match for you."

Because Cyrus was right, I didn't reply, even though he was talking as if we were in a Regency novel.

I just sighed, tipped some more incense into the stone holder, and prepared to cleanse Mom's crystal ball.

Again.

5

I centered myself, slowed my breathing down, and called Rhiannon over to my side. She jumped up on the makeshift altar, positioning herself so she could gaze into the crystal, too. This was something we'd been meaning to practice but hadn't gotten around to yet. I had a hunch that Rhiannon would see things in the orb I couldn't, and vice versa. My hope was that by pooling information, both our visions would grow stronger and more effective.

Reaching behind myself for another sliver of kindling, I was about to light the tapers when a pounding sounded at the front door.

"On it," Stefon said, leaping up again. He's always happiest when he feels useful.

I groaned. Was I not meant to consult the crystal ball tonight? Did the answers to the riddle of the lost elf lie elsewhere? Was that what was happening?

Cyrus seemed unconcerned by any of this, one foot

crossed over a knee, calmly sipping wine and staring off into space.

With a clatter, Delta Crabbit entered, with Preston the gnome sticking his chubby little head up from the padded tote bag she always carried him in. Preston's apple cheeks were pink with cold, and I hoped there was a blanket in that thing. His purple hat had red trim today. I'd have to ask him if he embroidered the felt caps himself, or if some gnome craftsperson did it for him.

"Sarah!" Delta shouted. "Pay attention!"

The older witch stood in front of me, bristling with anger. She shucked an orange wool hat with a pink tassel off her head and I winced at the dreadful color combination.

"Did Preston pick that hat out?" I asked.

She scowled at me, short gray hair sticking out on end all over her head.

"What kind of question is that at a time like this?" she said.

"Yes!" Preston said at the same time. "Do you like it?"

"Uhhh…"

Delta opened her mouth, looking as if she was about to head into a tirade, when Cyrus clapped his hands.

We all turned.

"Thank you," Cyrus said, calmly picking up his glass of wine as if nothing had just happened. "Please. Every-one. Sit."

We all looked at each other, shrugged, and found our seats. I plopped on the couch next to Stefon while Delta and Preston took the chair across from Cyrus. Preston climbed out of the tote bag and perched on the padded arm of the chair.

"Delta, what happened?" I asked.

"That elf is a menace!" She practically spat the words.

"Now Delta. He is not! He's just lost and scared!" Preston sat, chubby little hands on his hips, glaring at his friend the witch.

"What. Is. Going. On?" I asked, putting a boost of Power behind my words. That got through at least. Both witch and gnome stopped and looked at me.

"Let's all take a breath," Stefon said. We all looked at him, incredulous.

"What?" he said. "You magic types are always telling everyone else to take a breath! Besides, it looked like you needed a reminder."

Drat. He was right. Everyone else seemed to agree as well, because I heard a collective intake of air, and the slow exhalation that meant we were calibrating our central nervous systems.

Everyone except Rhiannon and Cyrus, of course, both of whom were still calm as you please.

Almost as if they knew something we didn't.

I whirled on my cat and my uncle. "All right you two, spill."

Cyrus took another sip of wine, gazing at me over the bowl dangling in his long fingers.

"I figured you'd ask sooner or later. And Delta, you're half right."

"See!" She turned on Preston. "The warlock says I'm right!"

"Half right," Cyrus corrected her.

"Which means half wrong!" Preston crowed.

I rubbed my temples. I swear. All I wanted to do was a little scrying with my cat, followed by a long snuggle and smooch session in front of the fire with my man. Was that so much to ask?

"Cyrus?" I asked. "Would you please explain what you're talking about?"

And another knock came at the front door.

"What fresh hell is this?" I moaned, quoting the late, great Dorothy Parker, as Stefon rose to answer the summons.

He returned with my ex, Cecilia, her partner, Toby the nonbinary hob, and a small sprite with green wings named Rowena.

I rose and hugged Cecilia. She's a small, Japanese American auto mechanic with fuchsia hair, and sported a rainbow coat over all-black clothing. I used to tease her that she was a Goth Hippie back when we were sweethearts in high school and college, and her fashion sense, like her fierce sense of loyalty, hadn't changed.

Toby shifted nervously on their feet. The hob wasn't too comfortable around a lot of people, though they were used to us by now, so I was surprised to see just how uncomfortable they looked.

Must be something serious then, to have brought them over unannounced.

I separated from my ex-lover-turned-best-friend and approached the hob. Where the top of Delta Crabbit's head comes to my shoulder, Toby is even smaller. The hob probably barely tops four-feet ten-inches, shorter than Cecilia's five-four. Stefon and I looked like giants next to all three, with Cyrus standing in like a lanky tree.

"What's wrong, Toby?" I asked.

The hob had dark brown hair and light brown skin and wore a green jacket over brown jeans and boots. Their usually unlined face was pinched with worry.

"The chaneques are upset again. They say someone is dumping magical creatures all through town."

"What?" I asked. The chaneques are small, stocky garden spirits that help Mr. Vargas in his gardening business and keep the garden near the tamale parlor in tip-top shape. They are often the first to know when things go wrong with what I think of as the smaller fae beings in town.

"We saw them, Sarah," Cecilia butted in. "There was a mini unicorn and some sort of butterfly lady."

"Not a sprite," Rowena chimed in. "But one of the rare classes of Butterfly Fae."

"They were both wandering near The Historic Kelpie Inn and seemed lost and confused. Mr. Vargas and the chaneques loaded them into the back of his truck. They're at the tamale parlor now, with Mrs. Vargas, Mr. Vargas, and David."

I looked to Uncle Cyrus for confirmation.

He'd discarded his wine on my not-going-to-be-used altar and his fingers were steepled in front of his face. He nodded at me.

"That was what I came to tell you. The Council suspects there's a fae-napper on the loose."

"A fae. Napper." Stefon's voice was incredulous. He's

seen some strange things during his time with me, and it looked as if he was about to see more.

"Do you all want to sit down?" I asked. "Fill us in?"

Cecilia shook her head, fuchsia hair swinging back and forth. The hob shook their head, too.

"No time," Cecilia said. "The Vargases specifically requested that you come, as quickly as possible."

I sighed, looking longingly at my mother's crystal ball. The evening was supposed to have been relatively simple. I was secure in the knowledge that the gargoyles would take good care of the wandering elf, though I shuddered to think what Duncan would find in the shop kitchenette when he opened up the next morning.

I had been fully prepared to do some exploratory visioning, get a good night's sleep, and find the answers when I woke up.

A witch can dream, right?

"Mrs. Vargas said to tell you she's been cooking up your favorites." Cecilia wheedled.

I cracked. Mrs. Vargas's cooking could bust through any bad mood. Even if it was a bribe.

And even if this whole situation had grown more complicated than I wanted to dwell on.

If I had to deal with yet another bad actor in the magical world? At least I'd be fortified with tamales.

"All right," I said. "Let's go."

6

Luckily for me, Mrs. Vargas insisted that Davíd serve us all food before the discussion began.

We all gathered around shoved-together tables draped in bright woven serapes covered by protective glass tops. At the center of the tables was a bewildering, mouthwatering array of food.

The only thing missing were the margaritas, though given the seriousness of the discussion to come, I guess that was all for the good. Alcohol dulls the psychic senses, making it more difficult to assess what's really going on.

I gratefully tucked into chicken tamales, green salad, and Mrs. Vargas's amazingly savory beans and rice. Everyone else seemed to agree that it was food first, but we were all eating more quickly than I liked, ready to get to the discussion at hand.

Finally, when my plate was half empty, Mrs. Vargas herself decided we'd eaten enough to start.

A short, curvy, middle-aged woman with silver-shot

dark curly hair, fabulously shaped eyebrows, and cat's-eye glasses that hung from a chain around her neck, Mrs. Vargas was a force to be reckoned with. With or without her apron on.

She rapped her knuckles on the glass table covering, and I practically felt the chewing slow around me. I certainly slowed down, and mid-bite on chicken tamales smothered in red sauce? That's no easy feat, let me tell you.

"Hector," she said, looking at her husband. I don't think I'd ever heard his first name. Since I'd known the family since my childhood, they'd only ever been Mr. and Mrs. Vargas, though I found out recently Mrs. Vargas was Ernestina. At any rate, their son, Davíd, and I grew up together, and my parents always taught me to call adults by their last names.

Mr. Vargas nodded at his wife, rose, and hurried off to the rock garden just off the patio outside.

"Should we follow him?" I asked Davíd, who was sitting to my right. Stefon was at my left but had focused back on his plate of food.

I didn't blame him. I was loathe to leave Mrs. Vargas's dinner myself.

Luckily, Davíd shook his head. "No. He'll come back with the creatures. It is all arranged."

Taking another bite of tamale while I had the chance, I chewed in ecstasy, then looked around the table. Toby and Cecilia had their heads together, conferring about something with whispers and gesticulations. Uncle Cyrus had put away a modest amount of food and was now sipping at a glass of water. Delta Crabbit and Preston the gnome both looked worriedly at the door where Mr. Vargas had exited.

Mrs. Vargas looked calm as you please, completely in her power. Every once in a while, I wondered if she was some sort of witch. She certainly worked magic in the kitchen, and Mr. Vargas worked magic with the gardens. Both of them had alliances with magical beings who lived around the tamale parlor and in the forests and gardens around town.

So, I answered my own question. They both had some sort of magic, but likely what my parents called the "small magics" that ordinary humans worked with every day, mostly without realizing it. These were the same quiet talents I was helping Tabitha cultivate. Just because she wasn't born a witch didn't mean she couldn't develop her own sort of power.

Besides, with vampires for parents, who knew what she would grow into? And done correctly, with enough will and intention, Wiccan rituals can pack quite the punch.

Every head snapped toward the sound of the door opening. Tiny hoofbeats rang across the broad red floor tiles.

Then I gasped, and I was not the only one. Encouraged along by Mr. Vargas, a tiny, snow-white unicorn trotted through the restaurant. Its horn was a gleaming spire of shimmering pearly pinks, blues, and golds. The magical animal looked like a strange cross between a pony and a goat, with all the best features of both.

And riding on its back was a small, perfectly proportioned woman, around one foot tall, if I had to guess. Her skin was pale orange, her lips and nose full, her cheek-bones high. Black hair shot through with flames of orange flowed in two long braids down her back between two monarch butterfly wings.

Oh. And she was totally naked.

Despite Rowena saying the butterfly woman wasn't a sprite, that was what I had been expecting. A tiny, fae creature about the size of one of Stefon's hands, not a twelve-inch-tall naked warrior who looked like she could kick serious butt with a single flash of her eyes.

Cyrus stood and bowed to both creatures. I had never seen him do that for anyone, and I elbowed Stefon in his gut.

"Did you see that?"

"Must be magic royalty," he murmured, voice tinged with awe. Stefon knows royalty when he sees it, even if it is just the hobbyist kind. His instincts must have taken over, because he shoved his chair back, rounded the table, and dropped to one knee, head bowed.

Everyone else at the table looked around wildly, except Mrs. Vargas, who sat and smiled, looking a bit smug.

Then everyone except Mrs. Vargas followed Cyrus and Stefon's lead, either bowing or taking a knee.

I chose to bow. Like I said, I haven't been jogging much lately and my jeans were half a size too tight right now. I worried about kneeling on the floor and getting up again with any grace.

The monarch lady waved a small orange hand, signaling for everyone to rise.

"Welcome, your grace," Uncle Cyrus said. "I have not seen your like in many years."

She speared my uncle with a piercing look, clearly assessing his magic.

"No. You would not have. We retreated a long time ago. How the scoundrel even found us, I know not. It is up to you to discover his lair."

The scoundrel...who was she even talking about?

Cyrus nodded gravely, then, to my horror, swept a hand my way.

"May I present my Goddess niece, Sarah Endora Braxton? She is Justice here and can be of help to you. My name is Cyrus and I am also at your service."

Huh. She got my full name, but he only gave her his first. What the heck was that about? If it was one of those names-have-power things, had my own uncle just thrown me under the proverbial bus?

Stefon looked at me with questions in his dark eyes, and so did Cecilia. I just shrugged and moved toward the little unicorn and the monarch butterfly lady. Too late now. She had my name.

But not the secret name my parents whispered in my ear at my seventh birthday. I don't think Cyrus knew that name, and now he probably never would.

The monarch lady was still looking at me. Oops. Guess I needed to say something.

"Errr...my uncle is correct. My friends and I will offer you whatever help we can to get to the bottom of this. Would you care to be seated and tell us your story?"

David was at my side, chair and booster seat at the ready. The unicorn trotted forth, and the butterfly woman climbed from its snowy back to the tall seat. Mrs. Vargas set down a bread plate filled with her tastiest morsels, then snapped her fingers at Davíd, who scurried to the kitchen and returned with a small napkin and a cutlery set that looked as if it came from a child's toy kitchen. He also held a ceramic bowl filled with what looked like milk, but was probably horchata, my favorite sweet rice drink.

He set the utensils down next to the monarch lady and the bowl on the floor for the unicorn, who lapped at it gratefully.

The little orange woman took one delicate bite of grilled squash, chewed, swallowed, then set the fork and knife down, inclining her head at Mrs. Vargas, who inclined her head right back.

Okay. I was definitely going to grill Davíd about his mother later. Clearly some ceremonial thing had just happened, and I wanted to know why Mrs. Vargas knew to do that.

But first...

Cyrus and I sat back down, and everyone else did, too. I cleared my throat, breaking the silence.

"Forgive me for not know the proper way to address you. Your Grace?" I began. She nodded in reply. Okay, not a fan of titles, but I would roll with it. For now. "But what can you tell us about this scoundrel? The more information you can give us, the quicker we can find and stop him."

The orange monarch lady threw back her little head and laughed and laughed and laughed.

"Oh, you sweet child, I do not want him stopped. I

want him found. I have plans for him, you see. I wish to foil the jolly old elf, once and for all."

"Did she just say she wants to take out Santa?" Stefon whispered.

I just shook my head. I had no idea.

All I knew was this whole situation had gone from weird to worse. And I hadn't even gotten to finish my tamales.

"I don't understand," I sputtered. "I thought someone was kidnapping fae creatures and dropping them around town."

"Oh, it is a much larger, more important situation than that," the monarch lady replied. She still hadn't told me what we should call her, so monarch lady it was.

"Can you explain further?" Uncle Cyrus chimed in. I shot him a grateful look, glad to not be the only authority type figure around the table.

Toby the hob shrunk into Cecilia's side, looking terrified. Cecilia had an arm around Toby, holding them close, a fierce look on her face. I didn't see Rowena the sprite anywhere, and the purple tip of Preston's hat was all I could see poking out of Delta's bag again.

Uh oh. If the actual magical and fae beings were retreating, this monarch person was either very powerful, or bad news, or both.

Looking at Toby, I realized I'd been calling the monarch "lady" and "woman," but I had no clue what her actual gender was. It could be hard enough to tell with humans, let alone magical creatures who had their own social customs.

I really wished the monarch would tell us what to call her. Him. Them.

Sigh. I was gonna stick with lady for now, because otherwise I'd do my brain in.

Luckily, the monarch hadn't noticed me examining her. Her attention was still on Uncle Cyrus, clearly responding to his power and to the fact that he's handsome as heck.

"We were plucked from our rightful realms, it is true," she said, "and there is a dastardly bounder stealing away fae creatures as we speak, hiding in the cover of a magical mist that we have yet to penetrate. Therefore, we must appeal to you for help. Though I must say, a day when my kind resorted to petitioning witches and warlocks for aid is a day I never thought would come."

I didn't know whether to be insulted or fascinated, but was leaning toward insulted. She didn't say witches and warlocks with any sort of respect. We may as well have been circus clowns or something, the way she looked down her tiny nose at us.

My mouth tightened, and I looked at my uncle again. He gave the slightest shake of his head, warning me not to tangle with the orange creature.

I sighed, and forced myself to relax, but as I sank into my breathing, I drew up some extra shields around my aura, just in case. Stefon straightened up beside me, pulling on what I sometimes teased was his "knightly glamour." He has a strange magic all his own, my boyfriend, though he would swear he was ordinary, through and through.

"Yet here you are," I replied, keeping my voice calm. "So, again, how can we help?"

Her tiny head snapped my way, and I felt her probe the edges of my aura. She smirked. Was that because she knew I'd shored up my protections, or because she saw cracks?

"Lily?" she said.

I looked from Cyrus to Stefon to Delta. We were all clearly confused. Everyone except Mr. and Mrs. Vargas. We were going to have to talk later.

"Lily!" Her voice had a knife sharp edge that time. I sent a breath to my shields, giving them another boost.

With a clatter on the tiles, the unicorn lifted its head, horchata drips gleaming around its snowy mouth.

"Yes, Your Graceful Flight?"

Okay. So, I could call the monarch person Your Graceful Flight. A bit of a mouthful, though. And I guess the unicorn's name was Lily.

"You shall explain to this gathered host what our conundrum is and ascertain how they might be of assistance."

"Yes, Your Graceful Flight."

Lily's words were respectful, but I could tell he was humoring the monarch person, who I was beginning to think of as Meryl Streep in *The Devil Wears Prada*. If Your Graceful Flight wore clothing, I'm sure one of us would have already gotten a tiny coat and purse flung our way and been sent for coffee.

"I have other things to attend to," Your Graceful Flight

said with a sniff, looking from Cyrus to me. "But rest assured, I shall speak with you two again."

She beat her monarch wings three times, and with a dazzling orange flash she winked out. Literally.

I only realized my mouth was agape because Stefon placed his fingers under my chin and closed it.

Even Cyrus, the king of popping in and out, looked startled.

Mrs. Vargas calmly began stacking empty dishes to carry back into the kitchen, as if nothing out of the ordinary had happened and there wasn't a miniature unicorn standing in her dining room.

David looked shaken but followed his mother's lead and helped ferry dishes through the swinging kitchen door.

"All right," the unicorn finally said. "Who's in charge here?"

Every single set of eyes around the table looked my way. Even the people helping to stack dishes paused and looked my way.

I straightened my spine and looked that little unicorn dead in its big dark eyes.

"I'm Justice here, but in Seashell Cove we work as a team."

The unicorn looked slightly confused, but I felt my friends relax around me. That was good. And my words weren't a lie. Without my friends around me, I wouldn't be the Justice I'd become. Maybe working as a group meant I'd never get an invite to join the Super Secret Witches and Warlocks Council my uncle Cyrus and his girlfriend, Ah Lam Wu, were members of.

But that was fine with me. I'd rather feel empowered by my friends than compete to be a big cheese. There was a reason I called the Council by that ridiculous name, after all. They did important work, I was sure, but they were pretty hoity-toity about it.

Lily looked around the table, which couldn't have been easy, given his low vantage point, comprehension finally dawning in his eyes.

"All right. This is very unorthodox, but I shall comply with your wishes, Oh Justice."

Cecilia smirked at me. That's the trouble with exes who are now your best friends: they know very well when you're stifling a groan. I smirked back, glad to see my friend looking more like her sassy self. Even Toby looked better, now that Your Graceful Flight was gone.

"What do you have to tell us, Lily?" I asked.

The unicorn looked around. "Is there a platform of some sort that I could stand or sit upon? My neck aches from looking up at you all."

David hurried back into the kitchen and returned with a solid side red cooler and a turquoise patterned serape. He set the folded-up blanket on the cooler and set the whole thing at the end of the table.

The unicorn sniffed at the blanket, then nodded his shimmering white head and delicately hoisted his compact body up. His dark gaze returned to me, and I was suddenly glad that Lily was as small as he was. I suddenly didn't want to come face to face with a unicorn any larger than this one.

My rational mind told me when it comes to magic,

size really does not matter, but my lizard brain screamed that was a lie.

Lily looked pretty, but his power was terrifying.

Which begged the question: why did two such powerful beings need our help?

Lily responded as if he'd heard my thoughts.

"We need your assistance because tracking the Old Elf and his henchmen is too much for the two of us. Also, we need someone to ascertain whether or not the Old Elf is behind this plot, or whether one of his assistants has gone rogue."

"What do you mean?" Toby asked, their voice barely above a whisper. The hob was back to looking scared.

"I mean," said the unicorn, "that you are correct, and someone is kidnapping magical creatures, scrambling their memories, and dropping them in your town. But this is not a technique Your Graceful Flight considers in keeping with the Old Elf and his mission."

"So, it could be Santa, or it could be someone else. That's helpful." Delta's voice was dry with sarcasm. The unicorn didn't seem to notice, which was probably a good thing.

"Yes. It could truly be anyone, but traces of Northern Magic have been found on all the transported beings."

I huffed out a sigh. Stefon squeezed my leg in support.

"Northern Magic?" Stefon asked. "Like Old Norse? Heathens?"

Lily snorted and shook his head. I swear he chimed like bells and his pastel rainbow horn threw off a few sparks.

"Not heathens. That is human magic. Northern Magic is the magic of the season. The magic of snow and fire. The magic of spiced wine and holly. The magic of gifts and..."

I held up a hand. "I think we get the gist now. Northern Magic like magic from the North Pole."

Cyrus glanced at me and gave a sharp nod. Okay. We were so having a talk later, and my uncle was going to tell me every dang thing he knew.

"Then I guess we start there," I said to the unicorn, keeping my voice bright, as if I knew what I was doing. "I'll get the teens on research and the rest of us will decide on a course of action. For one thing, we need to ascertain if more beings have been dropped in Seashell Cove. Fingers crossed, there aren't any we don't already know of."

But it would be nice to be sure. I reminded myself that was how every single case started: in abject confusion.

Why would this one be any different?

8

Rain fell steadily outside the big windows of Angie's Blueberry Café. Stefon and I sat at a big table near the back of the place, waiting on the teens, Carol, Delta, and Preston. I'd dropped a complaining Rhiannon off at The Widening Gyre and told my manager, Duncan, I'd be back as soon as I could.

Rhiannon pretended to be miffed at missing both meetings, but really? She hated being out in the cold, and preferred either the bookshop or my house, both of which had comfy beds for her to rest on. Neither the Vargases nor Angie allowed animals inside, of course—except unicorns, I guessed—but I had convinced my cranky cat that the seats were hard and uncomfortable.

That shut her up. Temporarily, at least.

I tugged the sleeves of my green Sasquatch sweater down around my hands and clutched a steaming mug of English Breakfast tea. A blueberry muffin with a side of whipped butter waited for me on a plate, but I needed to warm up first.

Stefon was happily plowing his way through a breakfast sandwich and coffee, humming along with some nineties band I vaguely recognized.

I noticed the man who'd come into the shop the day before, his red coat slung over the back of his chair. You know, he resembled the classic Saint Nick... but was he? I made a note to keep an eye on him.

Big hands wrapped around a mug, he leaned across the table, talking intensely with another big white man with brown hair and a beard. The other man was looking a bit raggedy though, a rumpled, pale green shirt collar poking out of a bark-brown sweater. His beard was shaggy and unkempt, and shot through with gray.

Rumpled Shirt guy made emphatic gestures, responding to whatever Red Winter Coat was saying.

They could be brothers, the way they looked and acted. I wondered who they were.

"Sarah!" Tabitha's voice rang through the café. I looked toward the front door to see the dark-haired teen shuck off her burgundy anorak and motion to Tracy and Carol. The blond teen and her mother both unwound long striped scarves from around their necks and waved before getting in line.

The door opened again, letting in Jerry Hamamoto and his son, Ash. The Tarot reader and his trans son were relative newcomers to Seashell Cove but had already found a solid place in our little ad hoc magical team.

Just looking at my friends warmed me up. I reached for my knife, split my muffin in half, and slathered it with the creamy butter. Yum.

Stefon smiled.

"What?" I mumbled around a bite of sweet crunchy muffin top and blueberries.

"You look so happy when you have a muffin. And when your friends are here. I swear, you are a pack witch."

I swallowed. "A pack witch?"

"You know, a witch who likes her pack around her."

Huh. I'd never thought of it like that before, but I guess he was right. "Maybe that's what we should call our little group. The Pack Witches. We could get patches and T-shirts."

"Patches and T-shirts of what?" Tracy asked, balancing her own tea and muffin and the blue coat hanging over one arm.

"Yeah," Tabitha chimed in, plopping her egg sandwich and coffee on the table. "Isn't that our department?"

The teens were in charge of store merch, marketing, and social media, and as a result of their meddling, The Widening Gyre was in the black for the first time in years.

"Pack Witches," Stefon said, grinning as everyone took a spot around the table. "I told Sarah she liked her pack around her."

"Pack Witches," Tracy said. "I like it."

"Except I think of us more as a herd of cats, rather than a pack of anything," Tabitha said.

Now that, I could get behind. It felt right.

::Cats. Cats are superior. Who wants to live in a pack, like dogs?::

Sigh. When I first learned Rhiannon could listen and speak mind to mind with me, I hadn't banked on her eavesdropping from a distance. That was just rude.

::How else am I supposed to keep apprised of things when you are out and about?::

The cat had a point, but that also meant I would need to up my mental wards and protections when I wasn't in an, ahem, meeting that she could be part of.

A witch needs some privacy, you know?

::Hmph.:: Rhiannon said inside my head, but then quieted down again, which was good, because I did have a meeting to run here.

Tabitha had pulled out a notebook and began sketching something, with Tracy peering over her shoulder, commenting quietly.

I'd ask later. Taking another sip of tea, I was just about to start the meeting when Uncle Cyrus and Ah Lam Wu walked in. Both of them were dressed far too nicely for Seashell Cove, as usual, and their long raincoats likely cost more than I made in a month.

Being a warlock clearly paid.

Ah Lam, a petite Asian woman with killer cheekbones, perfect skin, and a waterfall of luxurious dark hair waved my much taller uncle off toward our table. He gave her a peck on the cheek and sauntered our way, his dark bald head gleaming in the overhead lights.

He shucked his coat, draping it carefully over the back of a chair, and sat down, adjusting his lavender shirt cuffs beneath the cuffs of his purple wool sweater.

"What did we miss?" he asked.

"Other than a discussion of whether this is a herd of cats or a pack of wolves or dogs, nothing," Stefon replied.

Cyrus grinned at my boyfriend. The two couldn't be less alike, in many ways, but they'd discovered they liked each other. Maybe it had something to do with being two of the few Black men in Seashell Cove. That had to create a bond, right?

But what do I know? I'm just a fish-belly-pale white woman with a just-making-a-profit bookstore, while they're both two highly successful, bordering on rich, people. So Uncle Cyrus is a warlock and a foodie and Stefon is a programmer and gamer geek? People with money understand people with money.

Luckily, they both like me, as well.

But enough of this. Ah Lam Wu finally reached the table, balancing two shots of espresso. Once she was settled, it was time to begin.

"Okay," I said, leaning across the table, trying to pitch my voice so it would carry to my friends but not the tables around us, "we have a strange situation. There's a monarch butterfly person, a unicorn, what looks like a Christmas elf, and who knows how many other strange, magical creatures poking around our town, seeming lost."

"Except the monarch butterfly person said they were deliberately stolen and dropped here," Stefon clarified for the people who hadn't been at the meeting at the Vargases'.

"Right," I said.

"A unicorn?" Tracy's voice rose in a squeak, and her mother quickly hushed her.

"Seriously?" Tabitha asked, keeping her voice low. "Can we meet it?"

They were both looking at me. I shrugged. "I have no

idea where the monarch person and unicorn are right now, but we could check with Mr. Vargas."

"I want to meet them, too," Ash said, a dark lock of hair falling over his eyes like a mini-emo kid. Though I don't think emo is a thing anymore.

"Okay," I said. "We'll see what we can do. But meanwhile, who has seen any beings who seem out of place? Unfamiliar magical creatures and the like?"

I wished Toby and Cecilia were here, but the classic car garage where Cecilia worked was busy, and Toby? Well, let's just say the hob doesn't get out much. Hobs prefer to stick pretty close to home if at all possible.

::By the way, the little elf still doesn't know who they are, but Petal and Posey are reading them books about the North Pole right now to see if it jogs a memory.::

::Thanks,:: I thought back to Rhiannon. That was probably useful.

"So, what do you need from us?" Jerry asked. The Tarot reader was shuffling a deck. Not because we'd asked for a reading. I think it just calms him down and helps him focus. He wore a hoodie with "Expand Your Intuition" on the right breast area. The words curved around three embroidered Tarot cards. I knew the back had the same image, much larger, with "Jerry Hamamoto, Psychic Reader" embroidered in cursive underneath it.

Like the T-shirts, totes, notebooks, and hoodies the teens had convinced me to offer, it was stylish and free advertising.

"What I need from you?" I looked around the table. Even Cyrus and Ah Lam were waiting for me to say something. "I need you to figure out as much as you can about the beings who've been dropped here. How many are there. What they know. What they remember. Where they came from."

"That doesn't seem like much," Ash complained. The young ones always want to get in there and scrap it up right away.

"It's important, Ash," Ah Lam said, tucking a long dark swath of hair behind a delicate ear. "Until we get the lay of the land, so to speak, we won't know where to actually begin. Think of it as magical prep work."

The boy nodded. He knew all about the preparations his dad went through before seeing customers every day. So did the teens.

"I'm pretty busy with readings right now, but we'll let you know if we find anything out, Sarah," Jerry said, slipping his Tarot cards back into their bag.

"Thanks..." I chimed in, after sending a breath to boost my protections. You know. Just in case anyone was listening. "That might help us figure out how much we can trust the monarch woman and her unicorn. And whether we need to go up against a certain jolly old elf."

Never in my twenty-eight years did I think I would utter those words. But if Santa was actually behind all this?

That elf was going down.

9

"I don't knoooowwwww."

The high-pitched little voice sounded very distressed, cutting through the clamor of the bells on the front door of The Widening Gyre.

"What's going on?" I asked Duncan. My store manager looked as if he'd been tugging on his short, bleached-blond hair and his black, heavy-rimmed glasses were askew on his chubby pale face. Duncan just shrugged, scowled, and pushed up the sleeves of his mustard-colored retro fifties sweater.

"Back there," he said, with a jerk of his head. "Elf."

Oookaaay. Clearly, he was staying out of whatever was happening.

I sighed. The meeting had been productive enough, with everyone taking on small tasks. Research. Reconnaissance. Walking around the shops and streets of town, looking for anything that seemed out of place...

I'd been hoping to come in to work and have an ordinary, profitable day. Frankly, I'd almost forgotten about the little elf, and had been looking forward to another cup of tea and working on more Solstice-themed book and gift displays.

Instead, I shucked off my coat, threw it and my purse on hooks in the tiny kitchenette, and headed back to what the teens had named "Biff's Corner."

It was the ghost's favorite place to hang out.

Biff, if you haven't met him yet, is the ghost of the former proprietor. He ran The Widening Gyre for decades before my dad took it over, but even in death, he never got over his love of books.

Who could blame him?

Biff was now a minor tourist attraction, thanks to Tracy and Tabitha and all their hard work publicizing our haunted nature. There was even an engraved selfie mirror with a ghostly shape etched in one corner.

But as I walked to the back of the shop, with its line of bookcases and a comfy chair with a reading lamp in one corner, there was no sign of the ghost.

There was no sign of Posey, Petal, or the elf, either.

Then another plaintive wail rose from the bookcase above my head.

Little striped stockings and black boots hung over the edge of the top shelf, halfway blocking the used fantasy section. The rest of the elf was grasping Posey as if the elf's life depended on it. The gargoyle wore a long-suffering expression on its stone face. Clearly this had been going on for some time.

Next to the pair, Petal adjusted the stone bow on top of her head, then glared down at me.

"Where have you been?" the gargoyle hissed. "This elf is having a meltdown!"

As if I couldn't see that. I did feel guilty, though. I really should have come back last night, or checked in before the meeting this morning, but frankly? I had hoped the gargoyles had things under control.

Or that the elf would have left in the night.

That last thought wasn't very Justice-like, I admit, but sometimes a witch gets tired. Especially during the busiest retail season of the year. Seashell Cove summers were nothing to laugh at, but holidays, now that the teens had the website and social media running full blast? Yeah. Holidays were crammed.

"Can you come down and talk to me?" I said to the sobbing elf.

He raised his little head, eyes rimmed with red inside the pale green face. Rather than making the elf look festive, it just looked kind of alarming.

But he unwound one skinny arm from around Posey's neck and began to scootch his little behind off the top shelf, boot bells tinkling. I opened my arms and caught him. Both gargoyles breathed sighs of relief.

::That thing is useless,:: Rhiannon groused, bumping my legs as I carried the elf to the comfy reading chair set up in Biff's corner. *::I kept trying to get him to tell me where he came from, and he claims he doesn't remember.::*

::Rhiannon!:: I thought back. *::Be nice! The poor thing is lost, far from home, and has amnesia.::*

"We want tea!" Posey's rumbling rock voice sounded near my ear.

I jumped, dropping the elf onto the chair. He

squeaked and bounced, looking up at me with big, sad eyes. I looked up to answer the gargoyle when the bells on the front door clanged, signaling the arrival of the day's first customers. That was okay. Duncan could handle them for a while.

Then the door clanged again. And again. And again.

I stifled a groan.

"Okay, you two," I said to Petal and Posey, "I'll get you tea if you keep watch over this one."

The gargoyles looked smug. Had they been pulling one over on me? Did they not mind watching the little elf? No time to figure that out now, I could hear Duncan's cheerful customer voice, loudly directing someone to the history section, which was perilously close to Biff's corner.

Crouching next to the chair, I looked into the little elf's eyes. "There are ordinary humans in the store. They can't know you're a real elf, okay? So that leaves you three choices."

He just stared, wide eyed, saying nothing. Was the thing an automaton?

The voices slowly came closer. Good. That meant they were browsers, and not in a hurry.

"One, you can sit here, absolutely still, and pretend you are a doll. Two, I can put you back up on the top of one of those central bookcases, and you can tuck yourself away, out of sight. Posey and Petal will take care of you. Third, you can hang out in the kitchenette."

"Posey and Petal, please," it said.

I nodded, grabbed his little body, and boosted it back

up to the top of the bookcase just as the browsing pair—an elderly white couple in hiking boots and bright anoraks—rounded the corner. Posey and Petal pulled on the little elf's arms, and his tiny boots tucked out of sight just in time.

I dropped back down to my flat feet, adjusted my sweater over my hips, and smiled.

"Welcome to The Widening Gyre! How may I help you?"

A giggle sounded from above my head, and the older man's eyes shot to the top of the shelf. I forced myself to not look and the man shrugged, quickly looking back at me.

"Thought I heard something," he said.

The woman poked his substantial middle. "I told you this place was haunted!"

She turned her eyes on me. They were a pale blue beneath silver-framed glasses that complemented her short, stylishly cut silver hair. "Do you think we'll see the ghost today? Or does it only come out near Halloween?"

I smiled. "Biff? He comes out whenever he wants to. I can never tell exactly when he'll make an appearance. But if you hear books dropping to the floor, it means he wants attention."

As soon as the words were out of my mouth, there was a thunk behind me.

Both people's eyes grew wide, and the woman shoved past me.

Thanks a lot, I thought, then heard Rhiannon snicker in my head.

I whirled, and sure enough, there was a heavy book on the floor, the couple staring down at it, and on top of the low bookcase that ran along the back wall near Biff's chair?

A black cat with green eyes was innocently washing her paw.

10

I narrowed my eyes at Rhiannon, who blinked back with an innocent "Who me?" look. Reaching down, I picked up a book on Scottish castles. Huh. Maybe Biff *had* thrown this book. It was one of his favorites.

Another thunk came from my other side. The occult and paranormal section.

The man yelped in surprise and the woman gasped.

"We come in peace!" she said, voice breathless.

I didn't want to tell her that's what you said to aliens, not ghosts.

I swiveled to pick up the next tome. It was a trade paperback with an elaborate Art Nouveau cover of the four seasons.

"*The Wheel of the Year: Pagan Traditions from the Past to Today,*" I read out loud.

"Your ghost likes folklore and castles?" the man asked.

I forced myself to smile. The store was full of customers now; I could hear them, wandering the aisles, talking to Duncan over some post-punk winter album he'd just put on. And the door hadn't stopped clanging.

Good for my balance sheet, not so good for figuring out what Biff was trying to tell me.

"Biff likes all sorts of books. He was the proprietor, you know!"

"Could we...could you...could you take our picture with the books?" the woman asked. "In front of the mirror?"

"Of course," I replied, leading them to the antiqued mirror with the ghost image on one corner and our store logo above it. Like I said, Tabitha and Tracy had done the store a world of good.

"Tea!" a gravelly voice hissed from above me. I didn't reply. The dang gargoyles could wait.

After snapping four photos in various poses, the couple headed back to the history section for some serious browsing. I shelved the castles book in the little end cap bookcase across from the occult and paranormal section, but when I went to replace the wheel of the year book, something stayed my hand. Something cold.

"All right, Biff. Message received. Thank you."

Biff wanted me to look at something in this book. But it would have to wait. Duncan's bright voice had grown a little brittle, which meant he needed help.

Now.

I walked down one of the side aisles, greeting shoppers, and straightening books, and was soon enough in the front, where Duncan stood, white knuckled, behind the counter, ringing up sales from a small family while talking to an attractive, slightly Goth white woman in a wheelchair. Standing behind her was a skinny Black man with a flattop punk-Goth haircut, buckle boots, and a black leather jacket that was nowhere near good enough protection from an Oregon Coast winter.

Duncan saw me, shoulders sagging with relief.

"Sarah! Could you help these, um, people? They have some very specific questions."

Great. That was our code for a troublesome customer.

I pasted the smile back on my face, thought wistfully about a cup of tea, and approached, glancing at the big picture windows framing our holiday displays, a gray sky, and the people rushing by outside.

"My name is Sarah. How can I help you?"

The woman backed her wheelchair toward the deep window display, as if to make space so the other customers couldn't hear. Okay. That was a little weird, but this is Seashell Cove, after all.

"I'm Jax," she said, keeping her voice low. "And this is my partner, Gabe. Do you have any books on reversing time?"

Alarm bells rang at the base of my skull, and Rhiannon raced toward us, nails scrabbling on the wood floors, shoving past customers who shouted in surprise.

Luckily, they laughed afterwards, seeming entertained. But the cat and I would be having a talk later.

She leapt gracefully into the window display, almost knocking over one of the Holiday Spectacular short story collections. The paperback wobbled, but righted itself.

As if by magic.

Perched next to the woman in the 'chair, Rhiannon began to purr.

::Do you know these people?:: I asked.

::They are legendary,:: Rhiannon replied.

News to me. It was funny, they didn't smell of magic, but there was something...off about them. And not just that they were a Goth couple in Seashell Cove, where Cecilia and Tabitha are the only two Goth or Goth-adjacent people I know of, since I put my black eyeliner firmly back in the drawer.

::Legendary how?:: I asked, but Rhiannon didn't get a chance to reply before I noticed the woman looking at me funny.

She was really cute, and bisexual me would have surely heard of her before now if she was legendary, right? She arched an eyebrow and smiled as if she thought I was cute, too.

Dang. Too bad I'm monogamous these days. I mean, I love Stefon, and am happy to be his partner, but sometimes...

The man cleared his throat.

"Are you okay?"

I jumped. "Oh! Yes. Sorry. Just a lot going on. Holiday season and all." I swept a hand around the store. "And my cat seems to like you. Her name is Rhiannon."

The woman, Jax, reached up to give Rhiannon a scritch behind her ears. "I'm sure we'll be fast friends."

But then all three of them were staring back at me.

"Reversing time? We have a lot of books on time travel, but reversing time? Unless you want physics books or something, I'm not so sure I can help you."

The two looked at each other and laughed, as if sharing an inside joke.

I crossed my arms over my chest, trying to not scowl. Seriously? I had things to do.

"Sorry about that," Jax said. "My grandmother was a physicist. She loved anything to do with time."

"Oh. Well, then why do you need a book from me?"

"Because..." Gabe said, leaning closer. He smelled of cloves and winter. "Jax's gran knew all about wormholes, spooky action at a distance, and bending time..."

"But none of her books tell us how to reverse time. And that's what we need," Jax finished.

I looked from Jax to Gabe to Rhiannon and back to Jax, barely able to believe what I was hearing. I wished Stefon was here. He loves all that nerdy physics stuff.

"This seems like a much longer conversation than I can deal with right now. How about we meet up later, for a cup of tea, or a drink, or something?"

Both faces brightened.

"That'd be great!" Jax said. "We're happy to spring for dinner, if you like."

"Oh no," I said, "that won't be necessary. Besides, I've got a couple of other people who should be in on this conversation, too. But meanwhile, please feel free to browse."

I turned to see what sort of help Duncan needed, when the door burst open again. It was Delta, looking frantic, her silver hair sticking out all over on her head.

"Sarah! You have to come, quick! Mr. Vargas needs your help!"

11

Luckily, the teens were both available to come into work early that day, so off into the gray day I raced, picking up Stefon on the way, with Delta and Preston bouncing in the back seats.

And I literally mean bouncing. The witch and the gnome were practically bursting with tension.

"Delta!" I finally snapped, "if you and Preston can't control yourselves back there, I'm pulling over! You're breaking my concentration!"

"Babe," Stefon said from the seat next to me.

I just snorted in reply, and my handsome, burly knight of a boyfriend wisely grew silent. As did Delta and Preston. I drove on, into the wooded hills just outside of town, though why Mr. Vargas would be all the way out here, I wasn't sure. Except...

"Hey. Wait a minute," I said, looking into the rearview mirror, where Delta looked quietly out the back window, Preston on her lap. The gnome's nose was pressed against the glass, as if he'd never seen a forest before, which was ridiculous. "Delta?"

The witch's eyes met mine in the mirror.

"Doesn't your family have a Christmas tree farm out this way? Is that where we're going?"

She had the grace to look guilty, at least, and nodded.

Stefon turned in his seat to look at her. "You do? Why didn't you say something?"

Delta looked at her lap and mumbled something. Preston patted her shoulder, then climbed off her lap to perch on the armrest Delta had put down between the back seats. I'd rigged a little seatbelt for the gnome back there—well, Stefon had—but Preston hated using it. Sigh.

"What was that, Delta? I couldn't hear you."

I scowled out at the gloom, tracing the curve of road with my SUV wheels, getting ready for the turnoff now that I knew exactly where we were headed, instead of the vague, hand-waving instructions Delta had given me before.

"I said, I thought you wouldn't come if you knew."

That was a splash of cold Pacific Ocean water on my face.

"You thought I wouldn't come? *You* thought *I* wouldn't come? You *thought...*"

"Babe." Stefon placed a hand on my shoulder, stopping me mid-sputter. "We get it. Let Delta explain."

I shook his hand off with a huff, but shut my mouth.

Delta's eyes looked stricken, and I exhaled my irritation, softening inside. Clearly, something was upsetting the older witch, and Stefon was right, I needed to chill.

"Delta, I'm your friend. We're all your friends. Please. Tell us what's going on."

My eyes bounced between the winding road ahead and the witch in the back seat. The energy in the car was palpable, as if the car itself held its breath, waiting.

"Something is killing the trees. I called Mr. Vargas out, to see if there was a blight or something...."

She turned to stare out the window again. I started to speak, but one of Stefon's big hands on my thigh stopped me. So, I drove on, and we waited some more. But I could see that we were almost at the long driveway that led to the Magic Yule Tree Family Farm, so I hoped she hurried.

"Mr. Vargas thinks it isn't beetles, or bacteria, or whatever else it is that usually attacks trees. He said it must be magic. Or a magical being."

Well then. That was an interesting wrinkle.

"Delta? Do you think the amnesiac elf came from your farm?"

Her eyes grew large as saucers.

"I knew it!" Preston shouted. "I knew that elf looked familiar!"

"Hold on there, buddy," Stefon said. "You mean, you've seen our elf friend before?"

"Preston?" Delta asked, voice quavering. "What haven't you been telling me?"

The witch sounded sorrowful, as if her best friend had betrayed her.

"I'm sorry, Delta, I wasn't sure of anything, so didn't want to say. I mean, 'I may or may not recognize a random Yule-slash-Christmas elf' doesn't exactly inspire confidence, does it? I didn't put it all together until just now."

"Okay, friend. I understand." Delta sounded so forlorn, I wanted to reach back and hug her, and we didn't really have a hugging relationship. Delta tended to be prickly and frankly, I probably was a bit prickly myself.

"Well, we're here," I announced, seeing the painted sign and pulling onto a long drive leading to a jam-packed parking lot with poles strung with festive lights, ambient winter-type music playing over loudspeakers, and a long building painted green and red where sales-people busily rang up people buying trees.

"That's a good sign, right?" Stefon murmured. "There are still trees to sell."

"Those are the newer crop, from trees planted five to eight years ago," Delta explained as I navigated my way between couples, running children, and a dog or two, finally spotting a parking place between a ubiquitous Oregon Subaru all-wheel drive in white and an ancient VW Beetle painted deep green.

"So what trees are being attacked?" I asked, as I unbuckled myself.

"You'll see," Delta replied.

Once we were all out of the car, I looked to the sky. The clouds were definitely threatening, though whether we would get typical Oregon rain or a dusting of snow, I wasn't savvy enough to know. The coast itself rarely got any snow, but sometimes the mountains and hills farther from the beach did.

Stefon held out a hand, and I slipped mine into his

warm, encasing fingers. One nice thing about my geeky, bearded boyfriend is that he's larger than I am. Don't get me wrong, my ex, the tiny Japanese American Cecilia, was a wonderful partner, but it's nice feeling the smallest bit delicate on occasion, instead of like a lumbering beast.

I looked around, wondering where to go, when I saw Mr. Vargas headed our way, his brown face looking very serious. A black watch cap was pulled down around his ears, and his winter work jacket was brown, as were his pants and boots.

"Delta," he said, pulling the shorter witch into a quick hug. Huh. Maybe she was a hugger. He looked at the rest of us, nodded, and said, "Follow me."

Mr. Vargas cut through the parking lot at an angle that allowed us to bypass the throngs at the white fences leading to the tree farm, leading us to a gate near the back that read "Employees Only" in bright red.

Mr. Vargas was a man of few words, so I knew better than to ask for an explanation until he was ready. Stefon and I kept pace, with Delta huffing just ahead of us, Preston bouncing in the tote bag that banged against her side.

"I feel like I should ask the little guy if he wants a ride on my shoulders," Stefon murmured. "But I guess he should stay hidden, huh?"

"Likely a good idea," I replied, but I agreed. That tote bag—despite the cushion I knew Delta had lined it with—could not be the most comfortable ride at anything over a sedate walk.

Mr. Vargas led us deeper into the farm. It was much quieter here, away from the shopping holiday crowds. It was peaceful. Nice. I inhaled the balsam-scented air and wondered why I hadn't come here in recent years.

Except I knew the answer to that question. My mom and dad took me here every year when I was a child. I hadn't moved back to Seashell Cove until after my mother's death, and by then? My dad was dying, too.

The life of a Justice is too often cut short. And I think I hadn't wanted the reminder.

We approached a stand of trees that were much larger than the rest of the farmed specimens. These were the sort of perfectly groomed tall trees bought to hold pride of place at the middle of a town square or shopping district.

Even though the handsome trees were still green, their branches drooped, and their needles were falling.

"Oh," I breathed out. "You poor things."

"Dang," Stefon said.

Our breath steamed in the cold air. Maybe snow *was* on the way.

Mr. Vargas looked at the trees, eyes mournful. Delta's shoulders were slumped in defeat.

"Delta?" I asked. Something worse than some dying trees was going on here, and I needed to know what.

Preston clambered out of the tote bag, looking toward Stefon, who held out his arms, plucked the gnome from the bag, and settled him on his right shoulder, where Preston gripped Stefon's coat collar and hood.

Delta kept staring at the trees, sniffed, and finally looked my way.

"If these trees die, my family farm dies with it. And so does my magic."

12

"You what?" Preston and I said simultaneously. Preston lurched, almost tumbling from Stefon's shoulder before grabbing my boyfriend's tight curls. Stefon grimaced, and quickly steadied the little gnome again.

I turned my eyes to Delta, my mouth agape. "Your magic is tied to these trees? But...but...you barely even spend time here! How is that possible?"

Delta stared at the browning, supposedly evergreen spruce trees towering above her, as Mr. Vargas scuffed the toe of his boot in the dirt.

We all just waited, though let me tell you, that was really hard. I alternated between wanting to shake Delta, hug her, and run back to the car as fast as I could. At least now I knew why she'd been so panicked when she burst into my shop. This was personal.

"Delta," Mr. Vargas finally said, his voice soft as a whisper. "You need to tell your friends."

"I will," she said with a sniff. "But not yet. And not here. We need to make sure the trees will be okay first."

That seemed like an order-of-operations problem to me. If we were going to help, I wanted as much information as possible, but Mr. Vargas quickly nodded and walked toward one of the sorry-looking spruces before I could say anything.

Stefon squeezed my shoulder as if he knew exactly what I was thinking. He probably did. That's one reason I was starting to wonder whether we should take things further.

Maybe move in together.

Preston sneezed, reminding me that now was not the time to ponder my relationship with my geeky hunk.

Mr. Vargas stopped in front of the largest tree, and now that we were close up, I could see just how badly off it was. From a distance, the trees looked a bit like old Yule trees that had been cut and left without water for a while. But standing a foot or so away, I could not only see the brown needles and drooping branches; I could sense the sorrow emanating from the trees.

"They seem sad," I said out loud.

"Yes," Mr. Vargas replied, as Delta heaved in a shuddering breath.

"I don't get it," Stefon said. "How can trees feel sad? And is that enough to kill them?"

"Of course, trees can feel sad!" Delta snapped out. "And sorrow has killed more beings than lightning strikes or sailing accidents."

Well, that was a sobering thought. And once I stopped to think about it, it felt true. How many people faded away from heartbreak or overwhelming sorrow? I shivered inside my coat, and Stefon put a big arm around me, pulling me into his side.

We all stood, breathing in the scent of spruce and balsam, the earthy smell of mud...and the scent of snow.

Sure enough, puffy white flakes began falling, melting as they landed. It was still too warm for snow to stick. Was it a good omen, or bad?

Or was it just December snow?

"What else can you tell us, Mr. Vargas?" I finally asked.

His dark eyes looked as sad as the trees felt.

"The trees felt very happy, just a few days ago. Then, all of a sudden, this happened. The soil beneath these trees feels disturbed to me, but nothing I do, not water, not compost, not singing...nothing seems to help. It's as if the soil has been interfered with."

"Like poison?" Preston asked.

Mr. Vargas shook his head. "No. At least not physical poison. But magical poison? The stuff you all are used to? Could be."

"Mr. Vargas," I asked, "do the trees here have anything like the dryad you were caring for?"

A dryad that had been murdered, we all knew. There was no need to say that part out loud.

His eyes darted toward Delta, then back to me.

She finally looked up, eyes rimmed with red.

"The farm itself is all the magic needed. My family has tended this land for generations, and I make sure to come out here every season to walk the land, talk to the trees, and make adjustments to the magic."

"Then what happened?" Stefon blurted.

Way to be subtle, boyfriend. But I wanted to know the answer to that, too.

"I'm a terrible witch, that's what happened," Delta said, voice suddenly fierce. "I have neglected my duties, gallivanting around, living in town instead of on the land. It's my fault the magic has gone wrong!"

"Delta," Mr. Vargas said softly, holding out his hands as the snow softly fell around us. "That is not true. The magic here is strong and old, and does not need a full-time caretaker anymore."

"Well, that's what we thought, isn't it?" Delta said, sounding on the verge of tears again. "But now, this."

She gestured toward the trees, then turned away, as if she couldn't bear to look at them anymore.

I couldn't blame her. I'd felt badly enough when the bookshop was constantly in the red. But when you were magical caretaker of a tree farm, and the oldest trees were dying?

That was a punch in the gut, for sure.

"What can we do to help?" I asked Mr. Vargas. That was why we were here, after all.

"Delta and I must do a ceremony to speak with the trees. But if you would use your powers as Justice to investigate who might have caused such a calamity, it would be well."

I scanned the trees, then nodded.

"Stefon and I can look around while you two do whatever needs to be done. Then we'll head back into town whenever Delta is ready."

I hid my wince at my own words. It was the right

thing to say, but this time of year, I needed to be in the shop, not cooling my heels at a Yule Tree farm.

Speaking of cooling my heels, the snow was falling in earnest. I was never more glad that Stefon and my size sixteen butt had finally convinced me that the cute little Fiat I used to drive was too small. My new SUV was heavy, and had all-wheel drive.

"I can drive Delta back," Mr. Vargas said. I looked at Delta, half-hoping she didn't need me to stay after all.

Delta was looking up at Preston, who still rode on Stefon's shoulder. She blinked, as if coming to a decision.

"Preston, I need to stay here for a while. You can either stay with me or go back to town with Sarah."

The gnome frowned.

"I want to stay with you," he said. "But if you think I will be of more use at the bookshop, I am willing to go."

My shoulders dropped in relief. I hadn't even realized how tense I was. Between the monarch lady—err...Her Graceful Flight—the unicorn, the amnesiac elf, and the holiday rush? There was already more than I could handle on my plate.

I barely had time to even think about honoring Solstice Eve, which rapidly approached.

"Preston, would you be willing to hang out with the elf? See if you can get more information?" I figured I might as well ask.

If Preston couldn't get more info, maybe he could at least calm the poor thing down. The gargoyles didn't seem too comforting, no matter how hard they tried. Besides, they probably needed a break by now.

Preston looked to Delta, and witch and gnome did

that silent communication that best friends or partners sometimes did.

"Yes," he said. "I will come with you. That way Delta can take as much time as she needs here."

"We can stay as long as you need, Delta," Mr. Vargas said. He really was a good-hearted man.

"Okay," I said. "Let's take a quick walk through the trees and see if we can pick up on anything, and then I really need to get back to the store."

"After you, babe," Stefon said.

He looked so beautiful with snow on his tight, dark curls and beard. I wished I could kiss him.

I wished we were just going on a walk in the woods during the first snowfall in Seashell Cove in two years.

But instead, I was stuck walking the woods trying to sense out what and who was poisoning the magic trees.

13

"What do you know about Santa?" I asked my uncle.

We sat in the dining room at Costa's, which was really the only place that passed for semi-fancy in our little coastal town. It was also Uncle Cyrus's preferred place to eat, which was fine with me, because he always paid.

No way could I afford their prices on my own.

"Why do you ask?" Ah Lam Wu speared a hothouse cherry tomato on a fork and popped it in her delicate, perfectly painted mouth.

Everything about Ms. Wu was perfect. The dark fall of her salon-cut hair. Her makeup. Her size six charcoal-gray suit and burgundy blouse. I bet even her magic was perfect.

Ah well. We can't all be petite badasses with expensive, well-tailored clothing.

Besides, Stefon likes my jeans.

"Because the monarch lady seems to have a beef

with the jolly old elf, as she calls him, and there's a Christmas elf with amnesia currently living at my shop."

And a suspiciously Yuletide-looking man running around town with what looked like his brother.

Ah Lam sat back in her chair, looking nonplussed. That was a first. She always seemed to roll with just about anything.

I stifled a smile and sipped my pinot noir. I'm usually a white wine person, but when the weather turns cold, I have the occasional glass of red. My internal smile was petty, I'll admit, but sometimes it was nice to know even perfect-seeming people like Uncle Cyrus and Ah Lam didn't know every dang thing.

"I can't comprehend why the Monarch of the Summer Sun would have any quarrel with Saint Nicholas," she said with a frown, a tiny vee appearing between her eyebrows.

"The Monarch of the Summer Sun?" Stefon asked, setting down his hamburger. "Sounds like something out of the SMA."

He was right. It did sound like a title one of his Society of Medieval Anachronism friends might bear.

"I don't know what the SMA is, but, yes," Ah Lam replied. "I thought it was obvious. It's in her manifestation, after all. She's one of the Seasonal Monarchs that guard the hidden realms."

"I mean, I know about the Monarchs," I said, because every witch does, "but I didn't think they could, you know, manifest in physical form in this realm. I thought they lived on the ætheric planes, doing their magic business through the actual elements the rule the seasons here."

I noticed I almost said, "spooky business," though I try to not use that word so much anymore. Too many other connotations. But for some reason this conversation brought to mind the reference the thin young Black Goth had said at the store. He'd mentioned "spooky action at a distance," which I vaguely remembered was a physics thing.

"That is mostly what the Monarchs do," Uncle Cyrus chimed in. "You're correct. But they have been known to appear in our realm in forms they think we can understand. Like fire salamanders. Or personifications of the North Wind."

"I never understood why salamanders are stand-ins for fire," I complained. "Salamanders like cold and damp."

"It's medieval, babe," Stefon quietly remarked, sipping at his beer.

"I know that," I waved a hand, "but you'd think we'd have updated the references for the twenty-first century. But before we talk more about the Monarchs, I have a question."

All three of my dinner partners looked at me, waiting.

"What does spooky action at a distance have to do with any of this?"

Stefon barked out a laugh. "Really, babe? Now you're talking one of my love languages!"

I poked him, but smiled. Stefon has many love languages, most of them pretty geeky. It's one of the things I love about him.

"Spooky action at a distance is how Einstein described quantum entanglement. That's where objects share a common state, even when they aren't next to each other." His face lit up and his hands started moving in arcs and planes, then picked up a saltshaker and his beer, moving them closer, then farther apart. I guess he was trying to illustrate the connection between two different objects in space. "Since Einstein's time, physicists say we can have that kind of interaction at even bigger distances than they thought before. Dope, right?"

Stefon was the only person I knew who still used the word "dope."

"Why are you asking about this?" Uncle Cyrus said. "How does it relate to the Monarchs or the elf?"

I shook my head, looking out at the dark, churning ocean. There was something there, but I couldn't put my finger on it. *Entanglement* was the right word, though. It felt as if a bunch of taut strings overlapped, then stretched outward toward different points.

"I'm not sure yet." I looked back at Cyrus, whose dark bald dome shone in the soft overhead lights. "But some people were asking about books on time shifts, and reversals, and the guy mentioned that spooky action thing."

Stefon chewed his hamburger, clearly deep in thought. Neither Cyrus nor Ah Lam had anything to say, it seemed. We all ate for a while, just the sounds of cutlery scraping on plates, and the conversations around the restaurant breaking through our silence.

My grilled-vegetable-topped seafood pasta was excellent, but I barely tasted it.

Then I saw the big guy in the tweed jacket sit at a

table nearby. He looked slightly less disheveled than before. I waited a moment, to see if Red Winter Coat guy was going to show up, but the host set down only one menu.

Dining alone.

"What are you looking at, babe?"

"That man over there. Eating alone. I saw him earlier, talking to the same man who was in the shop when the elf showed up."

Both Cyrus and Ah Lam set their forks down.

"Wait a minute," Cyrus said. "What man? What did he look like?"

"He was a big white guy, well-groomed, wearing a red winter coat with a sprig of holly on the lapel. Said he was buying gifts and loved books, but then he just sort of disappeared."

"Did you recognize him?" Stefon asked.

"No, and that was strange, because you'd think if he loved books so much, I would've seen him in the store before."

December isn't exactly tourist season on the coast, despite Delta's family tree farm being nearby. There were plenty of other places to get both books and trees closer to more populated towns.

"Unless he's here meeting someone," Ah Lam remarked.

"Yeah," I said, "like that man over there. But why would they meet here, of all places? In winter? And even though they kind of look like brothers, they frankly didn't seem too friendly."

Cyrus leaned across the table, voice low. "What do you mean, they looked like brothers?"

My uncle's dark eyes were intense.

"Well, see what that guy looks like? Kind of big, with the dark hair and beard? The other man looked similar. Both of them have white skin that looks like they've spent some time outside, both have similar builds and hair, though the man in the red coat didn't have any gray in his beard, and looked neater. More put together, if you know what I mean."

Cyrus and Ah Lam exchanged a look, and she gave a sharp nod, as if giving my uncle permission to go ahead.

I swear, sometimes it's like eating dinner with spies, being around those two. There's a lot they can't share—council business—and that gets annoying.

Cyrus sat back, and took a sip of wine, looking thoughtful, as if he needed to figure out how to say whatever the thing was he and his girlfriend just had their silent conversation about.

Speaking of silent conversations, were they mind speaking when they did that? Or was it just your typical close friend or couple kind of communication where words weren't necessary? Something to look into, I guess.

I sipped my own wine, too tense to eat my pasta all of a sudden.

"I think they're the Holly King and the Oak King," Cyrus finally said. "Come to town for some reason."

Stefon gave a low whistle. "No. Shit. How dope is that?"

"You mean, like the Wiccan stories about the turning of the year?" I knew those stories, but never figured they were real. They just seemed like fables humans used to mark time and make sense of the world.

"Exactly the same," Uncle Cyrus said. "And they are very real. I've just never heard of them manifesting in such direct physical form, have you?"

Ah Lam shook her head, her perfectly cut dark waterfall swinging back and forth around her beautiful face. "I have not. But, like the Monarch of Air, there seems to be a reason they are here, now."

Great. Just great. Powerful beings that didn't usually take form in our world were popping up out of nowhere, riding unicorns and shopping for books.

"Does the Holly King leave silver bells behind?" I asked, feeling the small knot in the front pocket of my jeans.

"Not that I've ever heard of," Ah Lam replied. "Did someone leave one?"

I scooched on the seat and dug into my pocket, holding up the small bell.

"It was in the holly bush outside the bookshop, right after the elf arrived."

And then I felt eyes on me. When I turned, the man in the tweed coat swiftly looked away.

He knew something about that bell, I'd bet on it.

I was just about to shove out of our booth and confront him when he threw some money on the table and scurried across the restaurant.

"Dang. He saw the bell," I said, "and now he's leaving."

"More proof that he's the Oak King," Cyrus said. "And

that there's a connection with the Holly King and that bell."

Really? But what was the connection between the monarch, the unicorn, the elf, and these two representations of summer and winter? Were they here to battle to the death?

And more importantly, what were we going to do about it?

14

Preston had calmed the elf down, though he had not gotten any more information from the poor thing. Soon enough, Delta had come by to pick him up, still not ready to talk about whatever was really going on. I gave up, closed the shop, and went home with Stefon.

Now, a new day had dawned, and I was hoping it would be more ordinary. Though I might need extra tea to make it through, regardless.

The teens were finally on winter break from school and were helping me set the shop in order before we opened.

I was grateful for their help.

"This looks great, you two," I said, taking in the refurbished window and counter displays and bright, festive lights. Tracy and Tabitha had also strung ornaments from branches Stefon and I had brought back from Delta's family tree farm, so the shop not only looked good, it smelled good, too.

"Why don't you put the kettle on and make us a pot of tea?" I asked. "I brought cinnamon walnut muffins from Angie's on my way in."

"I thought I smelled cinnamon!" Tracy said, bouncing in her winter boots as Tabitha placed one last ornament on the spruce bough hanging above the door. The thin Goth clambered down the footstool and brushed off her hands.

"Do you think we should put a garland or something around Biff's mirror?" she asked. "Would he like that?"

I smiled. "Why don't you ask him? He probably has an opinion on the matter."

"What," Tracy said, "he'll throw a book of Yule traditions on the ground for yes, and a book on spring for no?"

"He'll let you know somehow," I replied. "Now please. Tea. I need tea. And I have something to talk to you two about."

"Okay." Both teens scurried to the tiny break room as I finished unpacking another box of overstock on some of my indie bestsellers. There were a lot of my favorite authors in the mix. Anthea Sharp. Kristine Kathryn Rusch. Courtney Milan. They were fantasy, science fiction, and historical romance, because people wanted all sorts of titles for gifts, didn't they?

A rustling came from the top shelves, and a grinding and scraping sound that made me wince.

"You two had better not be scratching the wood up there," I said, not bothering to look. There was sudden silence, then Posey's gravely voice spoke.

"Your shelves are unmarred, as usual. We are not barbaric."

Well, no. But when you have stone claws on the ends of your stone feet, a few scratches are to be expected. Not that I'd let either Petal or Posey know I thought that.

"The young elf wishes to speak with you," Petal said.

Right. My other problem. I did look up that time, and saw three small faces peering down at me, two stone-gray and the other pale elf-green. At least the Yule elf's eyes weren't red anymore, which was good. That was a bad combination with the green skin.

"I think I remembered something," it said, voice tentative.

Huh. "Can you come down? We're about to have some tea. We can talk before the store opens."

"Okay," said the elf. Kicking striped-tights-covered legs and little boots over the edge, he turned and began carefully climbing down the shelves to the ground. Posey and Petal hopped their way toward the bookcases closer to the comfy chairs set beneath the stained-glass window of a pile of books in the middle of the stacks.

Soon enough, we all settled in, with the elf on one of the new seating thingies the teens insisted I buy for the young adult section. They called them poufs. I call them tuffets.

Potay-to, potah-to.

Tabitha and I sat on the chairs, and Tracy perched on the other tuffet, with the gargoyles lurking overhead.

Everyone—including the gargoyles—had a steaming cup of English Breakfast tea.

The little elf hunched around his tiny cup and sniffed, then sipped thoughtfully.

Tracy was jittering on her pouf until Tabitha glared at

her. It's funny, the Wiccan has more magical discipline than the hereditary witch. Guess that's what happens when you have to work three times as hard for a third of the results.

Witches, warlocks, and magicians can get complacent. And complacency makes us lazy.

Finally, the elf sighed, releasing a breath with a shudder that shook its little body.

"My name is..." It gulped.

We all leaned forward, waiting.

"My name is...Melchior."

"Melchior?" Tabitha sounded shocked. "Like one of the Magi?"

The elf shrugged. "If you say so."

"Do you remember anything else?" I asked. "Like how you ended up here?"

"Some things are coming back to me." Melchior sipped some more tea. "But I don't know if they make any sense."

I settled back in my chair and took another fortifying sip from my own mug. "Try us."

"Well, I think I was working, because there were other elves like me around, and we were at long tables...doing something. I'm not sure. Then there's another scene. People screaming. A flash of light. Then darkness."

The elf looked at me, as if asking me to make sense of it all. It definitely seemed as if this was a Yule elf, likely under the employ of the Monarch Lady's Jolly Old Elf. But it still wasn't much to go on.

"Did you see anything else?" Posey prodded from above.

The elf glanced upward at the gargoyle, then back down toward its tea. Melchior shook his head sadly.

We all drank more tea. Then Tabitha spoke up.

"Sarah? Can you use some sort of magic to help the elf remember? You know, like hypnosis or something? Or past life regression, but for this life?"

I nodded slowly. "That's actually a really good idea, Tabitha."

The young Goth witch tucked a dark purple strand of hair behind her ear, looking quite pleased with herself, and I didn't blame her.

"Melchior?"

The little elf's eyes were huge, staring from me, to Tabitha, and back again.

"Will...will it hurt?" he asked.

"No," I replied, and that was mostly true. It wouldn't physically hurt, but dredging up old memories could be a painful process, emotionally. Our minds submerge things for a reason, after all.

I glanced at my watch. Barely enough time to do the thing before we had to open the shop. Magic doesn't pay the bills, after all. At least, not my kind of magic.

Though sometimes it helps things along.

"What do we need to do?" Tracy asked.

"Does Melchior need to lie down or something? I don't think that pouf will be very stable." Tabitha frowned at the green-wool-covered tuffet, and I took her point.

"Melchior can take your chair, and you can take the tuffet. All I need from you two is to keep your psychic eyes and ears open, and alert me if you sense anything going wrong."

"What about us?" Petal's gravelly voice asked.

"Keep watch. Keep guard. Make sure the shop wards stay intact."

I didn't expect any issues, but it wouldn't hurt to be extra vigilant.

Besides, that's what gargoyles are for.

"Tracy, Tabitha? Will you clear the tea things into the kitchen? And set things up to make more?"

We would need it after.

The teens scrambled to clear our mugs and bustled off to the kitchen, as I got Melchior settled in the big armchair that dwarfed its skinny limbs.

"You're going to be okay, Melchior, I promise."

The little elf sniffed again but nodded.

"I trust you," he said.

"Thanks," I replied, giving it an encouraging smile.

I hoped what I'd just said didn't turn out to be a lie.

15

I'd double-checked that the front door was locked, and texted Duncan to not disturb us if he came in early. My manager does that sometimes. What can I say? He's a conscientious guy, and I pay him well.

He makes more than I do, actually. But that's what sometimes happens when you try to be a decent human who also runs a retail store.

Soon enough, we were settled in the little alcove beneath the stained glass. There was no sun shining through it today, just watery gray light. I shivered in my sweater, wondering if more snow was on its way.

Melchior looked terrified. The little elf was stiff as a board, tiny hands gripping the chair arms, eyes wide, following my every move.

"Let's all go through some breathing exercises. It will help the energy."

And if I led everyone through the basic pre-magic warmups, the elf might not feel so singled out. Besides, there's ample proof that group energy affects every person in the circle. That's part of how covens and magical lodges work. Don't believe me? Heck, even Buddhist meditation groups and Jewish people gathered for prayer notice a difference.

"Close your eyes." I kept mine open for now, so I could monitor the elf. The poor little thing screwed his eyes shut as if bracing for a blow. Clearly, we needed to work on the whole relaxation thing.

A cool draft brushed across my face. Biff had decided to show up. Good. Maybe the ghost could help.

"Slow your breathing down. Take in a big, long, breath. Hold it for a moment. Now exhale in one long stream."

We all breathed together. After around four repetitions, I could feel the group syncing together. Good.

"Now, tense up as many muscles as you can. Hold. And release on your next exhalation."

It felt good to ball my fists and clench every muscle. I really needed to find a way to get more exercise in winter, when jogging outdoors became sheer misery.

With a big whoosh of breath, I released all my muscles, leaving them feeling warmer and far more relaxed than before.

"Inhale again and imagine you can gather your attention inside your head. Pretend its a ball. Now, as you exhale, imagine dropping your attention deep into your belly."

I felt as everyone complied. It took Tabitha and Melchior an extra moment or two, but they got it. Even Posey and Petal felt more centered above me.

Note to self: gargoyles can center themselves.

"Just keep breathing. No matter what happens, you can return to an awareness of your breath and your center. Now, Melchior..."

The little elf squeaked, and his big eyes flew open. Drat.

"Close your eyes again and return to your breathing. Find your center. Just relax. It's okay. We've all got you. We're all here to support you."

The elf closed his eyes again but remained tense. "B-but, why? Why are you here to support me?"

"Because you need our help," Tabitha said, a fierce edge to her voice.

"And that's what friends do," Tracy chimed in.

Both teens kept their eyes closed and their breathing even. The little elf's face screwed up in confusion.

"You're my friends?"

"Of course, we are, Melchior," Petal said from above. "We all want to help you. Now do as Sarah says. You're in good hands."

"Okay." The little elf seemed a little more reassured, but there was a sad tinge to his voice. I wondered what that was about. Maybe we could talk about it later.

Or maybe this regression would bring some more of the story out.

"Melchior, keep breathing. Slowly. In. Pause. Out. Pause. I'm going to take you back in time now." He tensed again. This might be heavy sledding, so to speak. "And if you ever need to stop, just tell me, and I'll bring you out. Okay?"

"Okay," he whispered, but seemed to relax again.

"Go back to before the flash. Before the darkness.

Before you showed up here. Imagine that you can walk backward in time, into your memories. It's easy. As easy as opening a door."

Melchior took in a long, shuddering breath, held it, and slowly exhaled. Good elf.

"Okay," he said.

"Imagine a door in front of you now. Imagine what it looks like. Is it carved, or smooth? Painted or stained? Old, or new?"

He frowned slightly, but didn't tense. I could almost feel the teens and gargoyles—even Biff—holding their breaths in anticipation. That wouldn't do.

"Keep breathing. Evenly. Gently. Slowly."

The group around me complied, deepening their breath and attention even more. That would help the little elf stay the course.

"Now imagine the handle or knob on the door. Can you do that?"

Melchior nodded, his right hand reaching out. Excellent.

"Now, open the door."

He pantomimed pressing down a latch, and swinging something out. Good. That meant the doorway blocking his memories was now open.

Or should be. What can I say? I don't do this sort of thing very often. Last time Cyrus had walked me through the process was right after my dad died and I'd locked away some memories of my own.

"Step through the door. Keep breathing. Tell us what you see, or hear, or feel."

"I'm in the workshop. There are other elves, hard at

work. Making tables, chairs, toys, instruments, all manner of wonderful things. I smell wood shavings and paint, and hot chocolate. I like hot chocolate. People are laughing and singing."

Melchior frowned.

"And then?"

"And then two big men arrive. One looks older than the other one does."

"Can you tell us what they look like?" Tracy asked, keeping her eyes closed.

"One of them wears something on a thong around his neck. A small, dark object. I can't tell what it is."

"And the other one?" I asked.

"He has a holly sprig on the lapel of his vest."

Whoo, boy. And hadn't I seen someone like that in town? Two people?

"Then what happened?" I prodded, making sure to keep my voice gentle, even though I was starting to tense up myself. I forced myself to breathe more slowly again, and to re-center and relax.

"Then the Jolly Old Elf came rushing in, and there was yelling and fighting and then..."

Melchior's breath was coming fast and hard now. The poor thing was trembling.

"And then?" Tabitha whispered.

"Then the Solstice Sprite came in, flying around our heads, spreading magic. But it didn't calm anyone down. It only made things worse. The Jolly Old Elf and the two men breathed in her magic, and got bigger and bigger and bigger and then..."

We all held our breaths.

"And then the Jolly Old Elf looked at you, didn't he?"

My head snapped around. There was Uncle Cyrus, backed by Ah Lam, both of them wrapped in warm wool coats dusted with melting snow.

"Yes! Yes! He did!" Melchior's little body trembled.

Cyrus started to speak again, but I held up my hand to stall him.

"And what happened, Melchior? Did he say something to you?"

"He told me to find a witch named Sarah Endora Braxton, and tell her he was coming."

I flushed hot, as if someone had turned on the heat full blast, and throttled down my anxiety.

"Breathe, Sarah," Tracy murmured.

I forced breath in and out of my lungs. It wouldn't do to agitate the elf. Not when I had to get him out of there.

"Thank you, Melchior. Is there anything else?"

"Th-then the Solstice Sprite shrieked, there was a flash, and I-I was here. I think."

"Very good. Keep breathing. Slowly. Now turn. Do you see the door again?"

The little elf nodded.

"Walk toward the door. Open it. Keep breathing."

The little elf pantomimed opening a door again.

"Now step through and imagine your spirit stepping back into your body. Feel the chair. Feel us around you. Imagine you can inhale from the top of your head to the soles of your feet. Exhale. Do that two more times."

I watched as Melchior followed my instructions and took myself through the exercise as well.

"When you're ready, open your eyes and stretch."

Everyone in the circle did, except Cyrus and Ah Lam, who leaned against the bookcases, waiting to speak.

Well, my uncle would have to keep waiting, after barging in like that.

Dang warlocks and their powers of teleportation and popping in where they had no business.

"Tracy? Tabitha? I know you just cleared up, but would you put the kettle on again for hot chocolate and more tea? But bring Melchior a cup of water first, please. And see if there are any cookies those two"—I pointed to the gargoyles—"haven't eaten yet."

The teens scurried back to the kitchenette.

"Hold tight, Melchior. Just keep breathing. We'll get you some water first, and then some hot cocoa."

"Sarah," Uncle Cyrus interjected, "we really need to talk."

"You!" I poked the air as if I was poking his chest. "You can wait."

I had an elf to take care of first. Magical care came before conversation, if it could be helped. Unless there was an emergency.

And if Cyrus and Ah Lam had brought an emergency to my door?

I really needed another cup of tea.

16

Duncan had arrived right after we got the little elf calmed down and back up on the bookcases with Petal and Posey. I left the teens to help my hipster manager and stomped down the street to meet Ah Lam and Uncle Cyrus.

Shucking my hat, I shoved it into one of my coat pockets after shoving through the door of the Blueberry Café. I moved to sweep past the community bulletin board when a flutter of colored paper stopped me in my tracks. It was a flier, ringed in red and green. "The Holly and the Ivy," it read in cursive script. "A tale as old as time."

But there were no dates on the flier, and no location of the event or whatever it was. A QR code was at the bottom right-hand corner. But heck if I was going to scan the thing.

Heading to the counter, I greeted Angie. Another big, beautiful woman, Angie had short blond hair poking out from beneath a blueberry-blue kerchief that matched her

Blueberry Café apron. Angie and had become friends and I valued her as a businesswoman. She was also a font of information about asexuality, which was an orientation I hadn't had much knowledge of before she came out to me.

"Hey, Sarah," she greeted me with a smile, but kept her voice low. The café was between the breakfast and lunch rushes, but you could never be too careful in any semi-public space in Seashell Cove. "What do you know about a guy in a red coat and a man who looks like his brother?"

My head whipped around and I scanned the café, but all I saw were an adult and child, heads bent over a coloring book, a man working at his laptop, and...wait a minute, what were the two non-local Goths doing with Ah Lam Wu and Uncle Cyrus?

"They're not here now," Angie reassured me, patting my hand that clutched my wallet on the glass countertop.

"But they have been," I said. "And you noticed something."

I leveled my eyes at my friend. She nodded, her round cheeks flushed. I unzipped my coat and sighed. It was kind of warm in here.

"They seem...off. Different. And as if they're here for reasons you should know about."

"What gave you that impression?"

Angie looked across the café and out toward the holiday festooned Main Street.

"It was the red coat guy. He tried to pay with a gold coin, and my part-time cashier said she'd need to ask me about it, he laughed and paid with a card instead. Said he'd just been joking and it was a piece of Hanukkah gelt."

"But it wasn't."

"Indigo said it looked real. And old."

Okay. That was a little weird. "Was that it?"

Angie leaned across the counter, eyes intent.

"Indigo also said the brown sweater guy opened up his wallet and she swore it was filled with leaves."

Great. Just great. Two magical beings trying to cheat local businesses with assorted faerie tricks was not good. And if I thought that was all they were up to here, it would be bad enough.

But it wasn't. Those two were up to something, and if it had nothing to do with the little lost elf, I'd eat Rhiannon's kibble.

::You keep your human paws out of my bowl.::

I ignored my cranky cat.

"Thanks, Angie. Ring me up a grilled sandwich and some tea?"

"You got it."

I paid—with human money—and threaded my way through the mostly empty tables toward the back library area where Cyrus, Ah Lam, and the two Goths clustered around a table, watching me.

Damn it. It was good to have confirmation that something was up, but when my barely magical friends were picking up on it? It meant that things were probably already careening toward the cliffs with no one at the wheel.

"Sarah." Uncle Cyrus stood and gave me a peck on

the cheek. I draped my coat over the back of a chair and sat down, ready for this day to be over already.

"Have you met Jax and Gabe?" Ah Lam asked, tilting her head toward the young white woman in the wheelchair.

"We were in the shop," the woman reminded me. As if the two of them didn't stand out in Seashell Cove like beacons in dark clothing.

"Hey," said Gabe, adjusting the stack of bracelets winking on the dark skin of his arm where he'd pushed his black shirtsleeves up.

"Hey," I replied. "It's nice to see you both again but...uh..."

"The San Francisco bureau contacted us on their behalf," Ah Lam said, dark eyes boring into mine as if trying to convey an ocean of information in one thought. Except she and I didn't have that kind of connection, so I wasn't sure exactly what she was telegraphing.

"I'm still confused. I thought we were meeting about our...issues."

Cyrus set down his espresso cup with a clink. "Jax's grandmother was a consultant for the Council for decades."

"She still is," Ah Lam interjected.

"Fair enough assessment," Cyrus replied.

Now I was really confused. "Someone please spell this out for me as if I know nothing." Because I didn't.

Angie arrived with my tea and sandwich, looked around the table, and leaned over. "You'll let me know if anything comes up about those two?"

I looked up at my friend. "Will do. Thanks, Angie."

Then I wrapped my hands around the mug and lifted the fragrant tea to my nose for a long sniff. Marvelous.

"Those two what?" Uncle Cyrus asked.

"Red coat and his brother," I replied, hoping that was cryptic enough if Jax and Gabe didn't know anything. "But back to Jax's grandmother?"

"My grandmother was...is...a theoretical physicist and witch," Jax began. Already I had a million more questions, but decided to put a bite of pesto, cheese, and spinach panini in my mouth instead.

"Cool woman. She doesn't live on this plane anymore," Gabe interjected. "She lives in an alternate dimension."

"And she's reporting anomalies," Ah Lam said. She picked up a coffee cup with one, perfectly manicured hand. She and Cyrus really were a matched, elegant pair. Cyrus may have been my honorary magical uncle, but it was clear he had not passed on any of his sartorial flair to his not-related-by-blood niece. Me.

I chewed thoughtfully. "Okay. So your grandma isn't dead but isn't alive, and she lives someplace else, and can still communicate with you."

Schrödinger's Grandma. Because we need more weird in Seashell Cove.

"That's about right," Jax said, poking at her bagel, which was covered with what looked like hummus spread and sprouts. "When it was time for her to die, she went elsewhere instead. Gabe and I visit her lab there sometimes, but we only found out recently about her connections with this lot."

Jax waved a hand toward Cyrus and Ah Lam. I hid a

smirk. Hearing two Council members referred to as "this lot" amused me more than it should. It was like an instant demotion or something.

Cyrus scowled, but said nothing, sipping his espresso instead.

"These anomalies are why you're here," I finally said, putting my sandwich down and wiping my fingers with a rough napkin. "You think these beings popping up in random places are connected to what she's sensing. But does this mean beings are popping up all over? Or are the anomalies concentrated here?"

"That's the thing," Gabe said, leaning across the table, intense look on his face. His eyebrow ring flashed in the light, reminding me of a lighthouse beacon. "Every single blip occurred in or around Seashell Cove."

"Gran insisted we make the trip up ourselves," Jax interjected. "Said she didn't trust any other form of communication."

"And you came into my shop why?" I asked. If they were coming to visit Uncle Cyrus and Ah Lam Wu, there was no reason to come to me first.

"The Widening Gyre is a hotspot on every map Gran has," Jax said, shoving her plate away. "There are streams of energy flowing out from your store to the other locations where there's activity."

I sat back. "You're telling me my store is the center of all this?"

"Oh no," Gabe said, raking a hand across the tight crop of curls that topped his otherwise shaved head. "It's not the center at all."

"But she said..."

"Sarah." Uncle Cyrus held out a hand to stop me. "Your shop is not the center. It's the place that connects everything to everywhere else."

"How is that not the center? And if it's not central, what is?"

Ah Lam looked me dead in the eye. "Delta's tree farm is the center. And your shop is the key that opens all the doors."

I didn't even have time to take that in when a clatter arose at the front door of the café.

Whirling around, I saw Tabitha, panting as if she'd run from the store, face pinched with fear. The pink pentacle on her black watch cap was askew and her eyes were wild.

She rushed toward us, practically smacking into the man shepherding his child toward the dish-bussing station.

"Sarah, come quick. A man collapsed in the store!"

17

Pushing open the door with a clatter of bells, I stepped into chaos.

Rhiannon raced back and forth, meowing as if someone had stolen her favorite toy. Duncan stood behind the counter, gripping a book in his white, pasty hands, thick, black-framed glasses on tilt beneath his shock of bleached-blond hair.

Books and holiday greeting cards were scattered across the floor as if someone had pulled down the countertop display racks. Because someone had. One rack lay on its side on the wood counter and the other was face down on the floor, where Tracy crouched over a large man in a brown sweater, pale green shirt, and a brown tweed coat. The face above his brown and gray beard looked hectic with fever spots marring clammy pale skin.

Above me, the gargoyles creaked, and Melchior moaned.

"What in Hecate's name is happening?" I asked.

Rhiannon yowled. Great. She was choosing *now* to become an ordinary, upset cat?

The bells clanged behind me as Ah Lam and Cyrus entered the store. Ah Lam immediately disappeared into the bookcases leading to the back of the shop, while Cyrus circled the other direction. Good. They were scoping out the store, hopefully making sure nothing terrible lay in wait back there.

From the back, I heard several loud thunks. Great. That meant Biff was upset, too.

"I don't know," Duncan said, tugging at his short, bleached hair with one hand as the other clutched his green Yule sweater with spaceships knit in rows across the chest. He looked positively sick. "He came in asking for books on trees, then his eyes rolled up in his head and he started making choking sounds. Before I could do anything, he grabbed the displays, trying to hold himself up, and then collapsed there on the floor. I sent Tabitha to get you and..."

"Duncan!" I put a shove of Power behind my voice.

His head jerked as if I'd slapped him, but he shut up, which is what I'd been going for.

Tabitha arrived then, holding the door open for Jax and Gabe. Jax wheeled in, looking around for a clear spot on the floor to park her chair. Tabitha and Gabe scurried around, dodging the still-pacing cat, picking up books and cards and stacking them on the counter.

"Rhiannon, stay still! And Tracy, please report."

Tracy blew a lock of naturally blond hair from her eyes and looked up at me.

"It was like Duncan said. The guy collapsed. But he's

breathing and his heartbeat is steady again. But something is clearly wrong."

"It's my fauuuullltttt!" Melchior's voice wailed from above. "It's allllll myyy fauuullltttt!"

I sighed. "Will someone help the elf down, please?"

Gabe looked up, his eyebrows almost at his hairline. But he didn't say a word, just reached up, black leather jacket lifting as he stretched to the reach the little green elf looking down at us, eyes rimmed in red once again.

Melchior dropped into Gabe's skinny arms. Gabe looked around for a place to set the small elf. Duncan and Tabitha quickly cleared a spot on the counter, next to a teetering, irregular stack of books from the floor. That pile made me wince. I hated seeing books abused, and hoped they were all okay.

Rhiannon leapt up beside the elf and put one paw on its little red clad leg. The two stared at each other, and the elf's panicked sobbing subsided with only a hiccup or two.

We were all going to need a cup of tea when this was over.

If this was ever going to be over.

"Melchior." I stepped around Tracy and the man in the brown sweater. "What do you know?"

"I killed the Oak King," the elf said, button eyes somber in his wee green face. "I didn't mean to, but I did."

"Nonsense," Uncle Cyrus said, rounding a bookcase. He brushed off his hands, which made me wonder what in the heck he'd been up to back there. Ah Lam was still nowhere to be seen. "First of all, the Oak King is not dead. Second of all..."

"I think we know why he collapsed." That was Ah Lam's voice. She skirted around Cyrus, holding out a heavy-looking tome.

"*Trees of the Pacific Northwest*?" I asked.

Ah Lam nodded, the fall of her black hair brushing her perfect burgundy wool coat. Flipping open the book, she held it toward me. "Read that."

I grabbed the heavy book and looked down at the page. My eyes widened and my mouth went dry.

"Oh no," I said.

The bells clattered again.

"Oh yes," Ah Lam replied. "I'm afraid so."

"Afraid of what?" Delta's voice cut through my reply. The older witch and her gnome sidekick had arrived.

"Blight," I said, looking around.

"But not just any blight," Cyrus said. "This is magic, affecting the trees at your farm, Delta, and affecting the Oak King himself."

"Whoa," Gabe whispered. "The Oak King is a real dude?"

"You don't pay me enough for this," Duncan said. "I'm going to make some tea."

I didn't blame the guy. Other than being able to sell more books to tourists than anyone I know, my manager has zero magic himself. He's grown used to our strange goings-on the past few years, but some things were just too much. I looked longingly at the back of his green spaceship sweater as he threaded his way toward the kitchenette.

I wished I could go make tea myself. But no. I had to deal with what was in front of me, didn't I?

And Duncan was getting another raise as soon as I could afford it. The teens, too.

"Someone please tell me how blight can affect two different species of tree at the same time. And tell me in no uncertain terms what it has to do with magical beings disappearing and appearing somewhere else."

"It's the butterfly tornado," Jax murmured. "And spooky action...and every other quantum entanglement thing you can think of."

As if I knew what any of that meant, other than on the most surface of surface levels.

"And it's all wrapped up in a big magical bow," Uncle Cyrus said.

"I still don't understand," I said. I made a note to ask Stefon about it later, but for now, I needed at least a sketchy idea. Other than the *everything in the cosmos is connected to everything else* woo-woo stuff that Wiccans like Tabitha believed in.

"Northern magic..." a voice rumbled from the floor.

The Oak King was speaking!

We all leaned a little closer, though Tracy scowled at me when I took a step toward her. Right. Message received.

"Northern magic what?" Tracy asked, keeping her voice gentle. This whole situation made me wonder if she didn't have some healing magic running through her veins.

"Entangled..." His brown eyes fluttered, then closed. But I had to admit he looked a lot better than he had just ten minutes before.

"I think I know what's happening," said Gabe.

"I think something went wrong either at the North Pole itself or in the legends surrounding it. That caused a ripple in all the magical realms. Kind of like an ice sheet breaking off in the Arctic affects fires in Southern California."

Unfortunately, that made as much sense to me as anything else about this situation.

"But how do we pinpoint where things went wrong?" Tabitha asked.

"And how do we fix it?" Tracy chimed in.

Those were the questions of the hour, and I might be Justice in Seashell Cove, but that didn't mean I knew the answers.

18

I snuggled up against Stefon and sighed. The fire crackled and hissed in the grate and the refrigerator hummed from the kitchen. Rhiannon lay curled up on a cushion near the fire. Melchior the elf slept sprawled on a second cushion on the opposite side of the hearth, his little mouth wide open.

I'd thought it prudent to bring both of them home from the shop, and our unexpected guest, too.

Down the hallway, the Oak King snored from the guest bedroom. He had roused himself enough to get into the car with Stefon's help, and then again into bed, where he'd promptly passed out again.

Stefon took a sip of whiskey and slid a hand down the arm of my sweater, petting the wool-cotton blend as if it were a cat. I purred and rested my head on his shoulder, enjoying the feel of his solid body and the scent of whiskey and boyfriend. Home.

"Do you ever think about moving in together?" I asked softly.

He shifted slightly beneath me, then kissed the top of my head.

"Only all the time, babe."

I jerked up. Stefon lifted his whiskey in the air, trying to keep from spilling.

"What?" he asked, eyes wide, mouth quirked in a grin beneath his luscious beard.

"You know what!" I crossed my arms over my chest and pretended to be mad. "You could have said something!"

He took a sip of amber liquid. "So could you, babe."

Well. He had a point.

I huffed myself back against the couch. "Where would we live?"

"That's part of why I haven't brought it up. I love my place and you love yours. I couldn't ask you to move…"

"But you don't want to give up your ocean view."

I got it. I live in the No View section of Seashell Cove, which means it's cheaper than where Stefon lives, high up on a hill. Leaving the home my father and I had made together after Mom died would be hard. And Stefon's swanky apartment was kind of small for two big people.

"We could get our own place," I ventured, tasting the words as I said them. "One with some charm for me and views for you."

"You don't think my place is charming?"

I smacked his arm, rewarded by a low chuckle. Rhiannon cracked open an eye and glared at me from her fireside nest. But she didn't say anything, so we must not be that annoying.

He turned to face me, eyes serious.

"Babe, you ever think of getting married?"

My mouth grew dry. That was so not the question I was expecting.

"I..." My heart raced and my hands grew clammy. Rhiannon snorted from her cushion. I ignored her. What did she know about love, anyway?

Then, all of a sudden, she was on her feet, back arched, tail thrashing, growling for all she was worth.

"Rhiannon! What is happening?"

Stefon was already on his feet, heading toward the small foyer to slip into his shoes and jacket. Next to the fire and down the hall, the elf and Oak King slept on.

I took a breath to center myself and cast my awareness outward.

"It's the monarch and the unicorn." I said. And something or someone else that smelled like peppermint and winter snow. "And maybe the Holly King."

"Call Cyrus," Stefon called from the entry hall. "I don't trust that crew."

"Call Cyrus for what?" my uncle's voice came from the kitchen darkness.

"Whaaz happening?" Melchior rubbed his little eyes and sat up, shaking his head.

"It appears that we have visitors, my small friend," Cyrus remarked, striding into the living room as if he owned the place.

"You including yourself in that visitors category?" I asked my uncle. I was suddenly tired and annoyed at the intrusions and the constant state of emergency. When was the last time Stefon and I had a proper date? It felt like a month, and that was probably true.

Cyrus ignored me.

::I don't like that monarch person,:: Rhiannon said inside my head.

I didn't much like her, either.

::When did you meet?:: I asked back, standing near the fire. I heard the sound of voices from the foyer as Stefon let our guests in. There was hoof- and boot-stamping and a harsh, tinkling laugh that must have been the monarch lady.

::We haven't.::

I stared at Rhiannon, but her amber eyes gave nothing away. Cats have their ways, I guess.

By the time everyone entered, my cozy living room felt crowded. That was mostly due to the combination of Stefon and the Holly King. Both of them were big guys. And the monarch lady, though tiny, had a personality as big as Stefon's stomach. Meaning, large. But not nearly as snuggly.

"Well?" she asked, once settled on one of the chairs near the fire, folding her dotted orange wings behind her.

"Well, what?" I replied. I crossed to take a seat sandwiched next to Stefon on the couch once again. The Holly King sat in the other fireside chair, and the unicorn knelt its front legs on what had been Melchior's cushion. The little elf now shared Rhiannon's bed. Would wonders never cease?

Rhiannon narrowed her eyes at me, as if daring me to say something. I wisely refrained and looked back at the monarch.

"What are you doing about the disappearances and all the rest?"

"What I am doing is waiting for one of you to stop lying to me." I leveled my gaze at the monarch, then the Holly King.

"Why do you think we're lying to you?" the Holly King asked, unbuttoning his long red coat. Sweat dotted his pale forehead. Must be warm because of the fire. Good. He could sit and sweat. Maybe that would make him talk.

"I think you are lying because something very big is going on between you and your brother, and it is connected to trees dying, elves showing up on my doorstep with ominous predictions about Santa Claus, and the monarch here who clearly has an agenda."

I so was not going to bring quantum physics into this discussion. Things were confused enough as they were. But the thought made me wish Jax and Gabe were here. And that they lived in Seashell Cove. The pair reminded me of myself and Cecilia not so many years back. Before I became a respectable business owner and took on the mantle of Justice.

"Agenda?" The monarch lady drew her small frame up and literally looked down her nose at me. That was quite a feat for someone her size. "My only agenda is to find out what is causing these anomalies. Who is stealing creatures and taking their memories away."

"Your agenda," said a new voice from the hallway door. Every head snapped toward the space, where the Oak King leaned against the door jamb, looking exhausted. The collar of his pale green shirt stood one point up and one point down and his brown sweater looked like he'd been sleeping in it. Because of course he had. Stefon had had enough trouble getting the big guy into bed and tossing a blanket over him. Getting him out of his clothing really had not been an option.

His beard was shot through with even more gray than before and his face had grown new wrinkles. The guy was aging before my eyes.

"Your agenda is to steal the power of Old Nick and all the rest of us. Your agenda is eternal spring. Your agenda is no Winter Solstice, no Diwali, no Hanukkah, no Kwanzaa, and no Christmas."

"What are you talking about?" the Holly King shouted as, simultaneously, the monarch sputtered, wings fluttering in distress.

I swear I heard Melchior gasp and the unicorn stifle a snort.

"I have told you that was untrue!" the Holly King continued. "Yet you persist in your foolishness...."

The Oak King sighed as if weary. "You are the foolish one, brother. How hard was it for you to win our fight this season?"

We all hushed, waiting for the Holly King's answer.

19

"I ...I thought you cheated," the Holly King said.

"And I gave you my word I had not. Brother."

The Oak King lurched into the room. Stefon leapt up and got him settled onto the couch. Oof. That made the couch too crowded. The brothers were larger than Stefon.

I rose, too, and helped Stefon bring out two chairs from the kitchen. I'd just settled back down when another knock came at the door.

"Are you kidding me?" I muttered.

"I got it, babe," Stefon replied, and padded to the foyer.

More voices as we all waited. The monarch looked none too pleased about the situation, but something had made her hold her tiny sharp tongue.

Cecilia, Toby the hob, Rowena the green-winged sprite, Jax, and Gabe all filed into the space, followed by Ah Lam Wu and Stefon. Then the doorbell rang. Stefon did an about-face and came back with Tracy, Tabitha, Carol, Delta Crabbit, and Preston.

"I need a bigger house," I said with a groan. Stefon raised an eyebrow at me as the teens brought in more chairs. That was boyfriend-speak for *maybe we really should get a nice big place together.*

Trouble was, I wanted a nice cozy home for the two of us, not a community center.

I'd thought my place was crowded before.... Luckily the teens, Cecilia, and Toby were all happy sitting on cushions around the coffee table. Delta, Ah Lam, and Carol took two dining room chairs, and Preston perched on the arm of the sofa next to Cyrus, kicking his little boots, which brushed at Cyrus's cashmere sweater. Cyrus did not look too happy about the situation.

Tough. He could get a taste of what my life is like on the regular.

"You were saying?" Uncle Cyrus asked the Oak King.

"He was saying a load of centaur excrement!" Her Grace was practically vibrating in her chair, orange-spotted wings lashing, she was so angry. Methinks the monarch lady protests too much.

"Wait!" said Tabitha, earning a glare from the monarch lady. She glared right back. The young Goth Wiccan had courage; I'll give her that. "First of all, I can't believe the Oak and Holly Kings are real. And are you telling me that the monarch somehow influenced the fight between the brothers?"

Funny the things we accept as real and the things we have trouble with. A North Pole elf? Fine. Sentient gargoyles? Check. Centaurs and unicorns and diminutive ladies with monarch wings? Also fine. But two of your neo-pagan legends come to life? Apparently, that was too much.

As a hereditary witch, I didn't much bother trying to figure out if my spiritual beliefs were real or not. There was too much I'd experienced from childhood on—including the untimely deaths of both my parents, meeting a group of centaurs, taking down rogue ghosts and magicians, and the fact that my cat could now talk—for me to be surprised by the existence of anything.

Other than bigotry and hate. I hoped I would always be shocked by those.

"I am not behind this trouble!" shrieked the monarch. "Why would I have come to you for help if I was the cause?"

She had a point, but right now, there was no one else around to blame.

"You are Justice, are you going to allow this slander to stand?" She leveled her gaze my way.

The ordinary bookseller in me was flummoxed and had no idea. But the power of the Justice in me? There was a glimmering...something was not right about this whole situation.

"Not one of you is telling the Truth," I intoned. Whoa. My Justice voice is a little disturbing. I'd never used it when I wasn't pumped full of adrenaline before, so I hadn't really noticed. And yeah, as the words exited my mouth, I felt the accuracy in them.

"You dare say that I lie?" The monarch lady was prac-tically spitting.

I held up one hand to stop her. The unicorn snapped

the air with its teeth, as if it wanted to bite me. Rhiannon walked, stiff-legged, toward it and swiped it on its nose. No claws, thank Diana and Hecate both, because that might have caused an international incident. Er...interworldly incident? Multiversal incident?

I'd have to ask Tracy and Tabitha to research the proper language.

The unicorn glared at Rhiannon who glared right back, standing her ground. The unicorn broke the staring contest first. Rhiannon sauntered back to her cushion and licked a paw with satisfaction.

::*Good job*,:: I thought her way.

She blinked her amber eyes in acknowledgement. The fire crackled. No one said a word. Waiting on me, I guessed.

"Sarah?" Toby's soft voice broke the silence. "Justice?"

"Yes?" I looked at the small brown hob nestled next to my ex, Cecilia. Toby was a hob of few words. When they spoke, it was a rare occasion, and usually important.

"Didn't you tell Cecilia that Melchior said, 'He is coming?'"

"Yes..."

Toby looked around the room, glancing at the little green elf who sat up straight and adjusted its little red cap.

"Then shouldn't we be looking for whoever 'he' is? I mean, don't you think this person is at the root of our current problems?"

"That's...very astute, Toby. Thank you for getting us back on track."

"That's ridiculous!" the Holly King blustered, cheeks

red above his beard. "Old Nick has nothing to do with magical creatures appearing or disappearing! How can you even think such a thing?"

"And who said we were speaking of Old Nick?" Ah Lam's voice was smooth as silk and cold as Oregon rain. "I do not believe we can assume anything just yet."

The warlock had a point.

"Who else would have sent an elf from the North Pole, though?" Tracy asked, her brow wrinkling.

"Remember what I told you about not all things being as they seem?" Carol asked her daughter. It was unnerving how alike the two witches looked, with their smooth skin and long blond hair. I had features from both my parents but was a carbon copy of neither.

"What do you mean?" Tracy said.

"She means that creatures popping here and there could have been yanked around by just about anyone," Delta Crabbit chimed in. Her short gray hair was sticking out as if someone had rubbed her the wrong way. "If it was only North Pole people, that would be one thing, but look at this crew. You think that unicorn has ever met Santa?"

Delta swept a hand around my crowded living room. No one had a rebuttal, but the monarch lady clearly had some harsh words she was keeping to herself. Fine. Let her.

"But the thing I want to know," Delta continued, "is what in all the nine worlds we're going to do about my trees!"

20

Everyone stayed for far too long at my home before Stefon finally growled and kicked everyone out. Luckily, he growled softly and used the knightly graces developed over his years in the Society for Medieval Anachronism, plus his natural charm. That meant that no one much minded being herded out into the winter night, not even cranky monarch lady. Of course, the fact that he looked deeply into her eyes and kissed her hand before escorting her and the unicorn to the door probably had something to do with it.

When Stefon turned his rich chocolate eyes my way, I was prone to agree to just about anything.

But between that meeting, the conflicting stories running through my head, and a slammed day at the bookshop, I was in a desperate need to clear my head. Jerry Hamamoto had called, saying he and Ash hadn't found out a dang thing, which was disappointing, on one hand, but on the other? I hoped it meant the only stray magical beings in town were the Yule elf, the monarch lady and unicorn, and the two big men.

The visiting Goths didn't count, thank Hecate.

Stefon was meeting me at the Vargas's tamale parlor for dinner, and I was looking forward to a margarita and warm, savory food. But first, I needed a walk along the cliffs. The cold ocean air bit at my cheeks and tugged strands of hair from beneath my jacket hood. I clutched the little silver bell in one hand, deep in my pocket. Walking the cliffs in the dark wasn't the best idea I've ever had, but I didn't care.

It was either this or go on a week-long spiritual retreat to sweep the cobwebs from my brain and my energy fields. And who has time for that during the Solstice rush?

Speaking of which, Solstice Eve was rapidly approaching, and I hadn't planned a thing. I should ask Carol and Delta about it. We should do something with the teens to mark the longest night.

I sighed, licking salt from my lips, and listened to the crashing waves below as I skirted the edges of the street-lights, seeking the shadows. We would mark the longest night together if we got through whatever this mystery was. My brain ticked over the variables as my boots picked their way over dirt and rocks and the hardy plants that held the cliffside in place.

A light flickered ahead, cutting in and out, tracing patterns in the air.

What the heck? Was some raver out dancing with a glow stick? That was not usual wintertime behavior.

I walked more swiftly, making sure to keep my boots

in good contact with the uneven ground. The last thing I needed was to twist an ankle, or worse, fall down the cliffside to my doom.

The light definitely formed a pattern. It almost looked as if the light was flying. In and out it zigged and swooped and zagged.

And then, over the ocean's roar, I heard sobbing. I quickened my steps. The light grew brighter and the movement more erratic.

Finally, at a rocky outcropping, surrounded by five chaneques, was the little Yule elf.

The chaneque are short, stocky fey beings who work with Mr. Vargas on the gardens around town. They make their home in a rock garden off the tamale parlor patio and communicate with a sign language system that I still don't quite understand.

Flying in and around them was the light.

I nodded a greeting at the person I thought of as the lead chaneque. He nodded back. His square dark face looked grim. When I got close enough to breach their circle, the rest of the chaneque backed off to give me room. I crouched down, wincing at the tightness of my jeans, and held out my hands.

"Melchior? What are you doing out here?"

"He said he was coming, but what if he never comes again?" The little elf sniffed and scrubbed at his pale green cheeks with one hand before dragging a voluminous handkerchief from one pocket and emphatically blowing his nose.

The light strafed my head, buzzing like a dragonfly. Or an angry sprite.

"Is this the Solstice Sprite?" I asked.

"Y-yes," Melchior snuffled. "She called me outside. Said she needed to get me away from human influences."

The light strafed me again, almost smacking my cheek. I batted at the air around my face, trying to stop her from getting too close. The light made a chittering sound that did not seem friendly. At all.

With a whoosh of my breath, I pulled up energy from the cliff below my boots and the dark winter sky above my head.

"Stop!" I shouted, holding up the hand not clutching the bell. I imbued the word with my witch's power and hoped it would stick.

The light stopped swooping and hovered in the air a few feet away, still buzzing angrily. It looked like a cousin to our local sprites, except it was white as fresh snow. All of it, from its tiny toes and fingers to the tips of its wings.

"Sarah?" Stefon's voice broke through the crash of waves and the murmur of the wind.

"Over here!" I shouted over my shoulder before returning my attention to the hovering sprite. "What exactly is your problem?"

Okay. Not my most diplomatic moment. But I'd come out here in the cold to clear my head, not get strafed by a tiny, angry being. And I did not like that Melchior was upset.

The sprite chittered and smacked its little hands together. Unlike our local sprites, this one did not seem to speak a human language. Or if it did, it was not a language I understood.

I smelled Stefon before I even heard him. Warm skin, cedar, and a hint of something that was just Stefon.

"What's happening, babe?"

His large frame made a reassuring bulwark against the Oregon night and the angry glow of the sprite. Melchior sniffled, though whether that was from cold or distress, I wasn't sure. Probably distress, given that the elf lived at the North Pole and all. Pacific Northwest winters are cold, but not down to subzero temperatures.

"The elf says it was lured out of the shop by this angry sprite here."

I stood, slowly. My knees can only take so much squatting on a good day, and at this temperature? I was surprised they moved at all. My hands were cold, too, because I'd left my gloves in the store. Forget a margarita, I was going to need something hot to go along with my tamales.

"Sprite? Huh. I never knew they lit up like that."

"As far as I know, ordinary sprites don't. Melchior confirmed that it's what the gargoyles were calling the Solstice Sprite. It must have powers that our locals don't."

"And the chaneques?"

I'd forgotten about the blocky fey nature spirits. "Not sure. They were here when I arrived."

"They don't look so happy," Stefon mused.

I glanced around again. He was right. The chaneques looked downright perturbed.

"Sarah?"

What was this, a cliffside party?

I turned toward the new voice only to see Mr. Vargas

heading toward us, hunched into his coat, a dark green watch cap pulled down around his ears.

"My wife says you are to come inside now."

"I want to but..." I waved a hand toward the strange assembly.

"The chaneques will take care of things. Bring the little elf and come inside."

I looked from Mr. Vargas, to Melchior, to Stefon, to the sprite. I really wanted to have dinner with my sweetheart and then to go home and sit curled up by the fire. But this sprite business was not right.

"Give me a minute," I said to Mr. Vargas. He grunted, clearly not pleased, but not willing to put up a fight. Yet.

"Sprite, can you tell me what you want or need so I can help you?"

See, I can be diplomatic when I need to be.

The glowing sprite buzzed and chittered again. And I still couldn't understand her. It. Him. Whatever.

Mr. Vargas crouched down and signed something to the chaneques. One of them signed back. The master gardener looked up at me, as did every little face below. It was kind of uncanny, but you know, this is my life.

"The chaneques say the sprite is upset and that all the winter holidays are heading toward ruin."

"Does this have to do with Delta's trees?" I asked.

Mr. Vargas nodded and stood once more.

"It has to do with everything. The two brothers, the monarch and unicorn, this elf here, and the trees. There is a sickness spreading and no one knows exactly why. Please. Let us go inside and speak of this over dinner."

"Can the sprite come, too?" Melchior asked.

"Lo siento," Mr. Vargas replied. "Of course. Any friendly creature is welcome in our restaurant. But if there is trouble, be aware that my wife will not take it kindly."

I bent to pick up Melchior but the sprite zoomed at my head again, chittering angrily. Trying to dodge the angry ball of light, I felt a loose stone beneath my boot give way. I overbalanced, turned to avoid crushing the elf, and all of a sudden, was heading down the side of the cliff, the silver bell ringing as it flew through the air, the sprite chasing after it.

"Sarah!" Stefon shouted. I felt his hands grab me right as something very hard, sharp, and cold whacked my head.

21

My head was killing me. But—I wiggled my fingers and toes—at least I was warm. But instead of tamales, I smelled antiseptic and a hint of vomit.

Lovely.

I fluttered my eyes open, got stabbed by too-bright fluorescent light, and shut them again, groaning.

"Sarah?"

That was Stefon's voice, at least. So, things hadn't gone completely pear-shaped. I mean, last time I fell down the cliff I ended up in an alternate dimension. This place just smelled like our local urgent care center.

"Wha' happened?" My words slurred a bit, but I didn't have the energy to enunciate.

"Apparently, your head struck a rock." That was Cyrus's voice.

I cracked open one eye, and sure enough, standing inside the white privacy curtain, my dapper honorary uncle stood next to my boyfriend, both of them staring down at me in concern. Other than being two Black men in Oregon, they could not be less alike. Big, broad, bushy, and geeky versus slim, sleek, and bald, they were the two men I loved most in my life.

Now that my father was gone.

"This mean no tamales?" I whimpered.

"Mrs. Vargas packed some up for you," Stefon said, "but I left them in the car. I wasn't sure when you'd wake up and figured they'd keep better out in the cold."

I pushed out my lower lip. Great. The mighty witch was pouting in the urgent care. Way to win friends and influence people.

Then I thought something. Something important. I jerked up, winced, and fell back onto my pillow, head pounding.

"Ouch."

"What is it?" Cyrus asked, voice intent.

"The Solstice Sprite. What if she and the monarch lady are enemies? What if this whole thing is a battle of wills and we're caught in the middle of it?"

No one said anything. I carefully moved my head and looked around the too-bright, curtained-off space. There was Stefon, and Cyrus, and an anxious Mr. Vargas, who kept turning his watch cap around and around in his hands.

"Where is Melchior?" I asked.

"Sarah..." Stefon began, then fell silent.

"Where. Is. Melchior?" I struggled to sit upright again. My head was really pounding now, and my vision was telescoping in and out, but in Hecate's name, I had a job to do and could not do it from this narrow bed.

"Lie down!" Cyrus said, voice sharp.

I ignored my uncle and lurched upright, scooting my legs to the edge of the bed. I prayed I could actually stand. Stefon moved closer, ready to catch me. I gave him what I thought was a tender smile, but given the shock on his face, it likely looked more like a grimace.

"I will not lie down. Not until someone tells me where in all the nine worlds the elf is!"

"Oh, Sarah." Mr. Vargas looked at me with wet eyes. "After you fell...after we tried to help you...the little elf and the sprite were..."

"Were what?"

"They were gone, babe. They just, like, vanished."

I felt my eyes roll back in my head and then I was falling once again. At least this time I hit something soft. Soft and squishy. And it smelled a lot like snow.

Cool fingers touched my forehead. A voice said, "She has a mild concussion and just needs to sleep some more." Was that a nurse?

I opened my eyes and was no longer in the urgent care. Instead, I was surrounded by white, white snow, evergreen trees, and a twee village made of one- and two-story stone and wood buildings with peaked roofs, windows warmed by glowing lights. The scent of woodsmoke and hot chocolate tickled my nose, making me wish even more that I was in my own home.

"Good. You're here."

"Ah Lam?"

My head was pounding and the warlock stood next to me, wearing a plum-colored wool coat that brushed her boots. Her dark, perfect hair was uncovered though, which meant we weren't really here. Which was good, because I wasn't sure if I was in my own clothing or a hospital gown. And no one sees me in a hospital gown unless they're a medical professional, or they've already seen me naked.

"I need to show you something," she said, and began half walking, half floating toward the village. Her boots left no prints in the unmarred snow, so yeah, we were in some alternate reality, or warlock vision, or something. I followed along, grateful that we weren't physically walking, because last I checked in, my body needed an Epsom salts bath, some tamales, and to sleep for at least ten hours.

We rounded a cluster of buildings and I gasped. Across a little square, behind a towering, lights- and ribbon-festooned spruce, was a three-story, one-block-long building that looked straight out of a European storybook. It had dark, Tudor-style crossed timbers and a stone base. The roof was outlined in lights, and giant candy canes flanked each side of the large wood door. A row of life-sized Yule goats lined the front of the building, red ribbons around their straw necks.

We were in Santaville. The North Pole. Old Nick's domain. And the streets were strangely deserted, despite the evidence of inhabitation all around. Except we weren't here, really. Now that I looked more closely, the whole place looked soft around the edges, and the slight shimmering that I thought was just Northern magic was likely because we were visiting from somewhere on the astral planes.

Which meant my body was still on a bed in urgent

care. But Ah Lam hadn't been there. So how did she hook up with my spirit? Via her connection to Cyrus?

But the more important question was: Why had Ah Lam brought me here?

The warlock was clearly not going to tell me, because she did not pause, not even to gawp at the spectacular display. Which meant she had been here before.

::*Catch up, Sarah, of course she's been here. Why else would she have brought you?*::

::*Give me a break, fur face. I have a head injury, in case you didn't notice.*::

Rhiannon didn't bother to respond. Cats. I tell you.

Ah Lam shoved at the large door, which groaned in protest. It was almost as if the thing hadn't been opened in months. Which made no sense.

A small foyer lined with wood paneling held several boot and coat racks. They were empty.

I padded behind her down the red patterned carpet runner, deeper into the building. I just hoped that we weren't headed for a fight.

22

Once we rounded another corner inside the large building, we entered a large, yet somehow cozy-looking kitchen, with a large green stove squatting between wood countertops across the room, flanked by copper pots hanging from racks.

The other wall held a white sink beneath a six-paned window, and wood cabinets painted with cheerful red geometric patterns.

On the opposite side of the room was a large fireplace with an iron arm designed to shift things on and off the fire. A kettle steamed from the hook above the low blaze.

But the star attraction was a large, sturdy table in the center of the room.

Finally, I saw why Ah Lam wanted me here.

And why the village was so quiet outside.

Half in a sturdy wooden chair, half draped across the table, snoring with all of his might, was a white-bearded man in a red cardigan sweater.

"Is Santa passed out?"

"He's been drugged," Ah Lam replied.

Great. Just great. A drugged Yule avatar and a quiet village that should be prepping for the holidays...

"Who did it?"

Ah Lam raised one perfectly arched black eyebrow. "Why do you think I brought you here? So you could do your Justice thing and figure that out."

She waved one hand in a circle at the word "Justice" as though it was an information-filled hat I could put on and take off at will. I wished.

I walked slowly around the table, searching for something, anything, to tip me off to what had happened here. There was a heavy, cream-colored mug of cooling hot chocolate with a half-gnawed candy cane sticking out from the rim.

A log popped in the fireplace. I jumped at the sound.

"Can anyone see us if they come in?" I asked the warlock, who was surveilling the room herself. She turned from her perusal of an open cabinet and shook her fall of hair.

"Probably. If they can see into alternate planes of existence."

Which only meant half the magical creatures in the known worlds. Some of whom probably lived here at the North Pole. But at least I now knew why everything looked odd. Ah Lam and I must have been accessing the North Pole via one of the astral planes or something. Kind of like a magical spy network. Which was pretty cool, now that I thought of it. And I bet the warlocks and witches of the Super Secret Hoity-Toity Council did stuff like this all the time. That's one of my names for the group, by the way. I refuse to remember the real one because it drives Cyrus up a wall.

A person takes joy where she can find it.

I leaned down and sniffed at the mug. The smell of peppermint and chocolate was almost overpowering, which meant any other smells would be masked. Clever.

Something shimmered in a tiny crack on the table, near the sleeping elf's pale, meaty hand. I leaned closer, but my breath only dropped it further into the crevice.

"Dang!"

"What?" Ah Lam shut a cupboard door and came to stand by the table.

"Something shining...but I can't tell what it is."

I pointed at the offending crack in the wood just as Santa snorted and shifted in his chair, moving his hand so it covered the shimmering object.

I stifled a curse when lights flashed outside the window above the sink. I heard the ringing of a tiny silver bell. Huh. I guess the bell had been the Solstice Sprite's after all.

"The sprite!" I shouted, heading for the sink and peering out into the dark winter night where the Solstice Sprite flew, tracing bright patterns in the air.

Wait. Not just patterns. *A* pattern. A word.

"Ah Lam, what does that spell?"

The warlock crossed to meet me, leaning against the sink, her finely sculpted face almost pressed against one of the windowpanes.

"C. O… Come home." She turned to me. "The sprite is spelling out *come home.*"

"Great," I said. "What do we do with the sleeping giant here? If he doesn't wake up, there's going to be trouble in another week or so. Plus, we still don't know who drugged him, or why."

We also didn't know what this had to do with quantum physics, the theory of entanglement, two warring brothers, a monarch lady, a unicorn, sick spruces, and a partridge in a pear tree.

"Breathe, Sarah," Ah Lam said.

I heaved in a breath of peppermint-, woodsmoke-, and chocolate-tinged air. Part of me wished I could stay here, in this place, away from trouble for a while. But I had a bookshop to run and people relying on me, didn't I?

"We have to dig that sparkle out of the table," I said, voice firm, already at the large wood slab, reaching to lift Santa's large hand out of the way.

"Stop!" Ah Lam's voice was sharp. My hand stilled, hovering just above the red-cardigan-clad wrist.

"What?"

"Does his hand look different to you than before?"

"What?" I was repeating words like a parrot. Great. Add a new nervous tick to my repertoire. That's what happens when I haven't had food or tea for too long. It makes everything go wonky.

But I heeded the warlock's words and looked down at the old elf's hand on the tabletop. It was broad and pale, and there was a callous on the side of his pointer finger.

"It looks like a hand."

Ah Lam exhaled in frustration. "Look at the skin color."

Then I saw it. She was right. Before, the skin had been pasty, almost devoid of color. Now, the pale flesh was flushed with subtle shades of pink and yellow.

Then Santa snorted.

"He's waking up," I said. "The drug must have put him in some sort of stasis."

"That's because it was a magical drug," Uncle Cyrus's voice said. I jumped and almost peed. "A physical drug would not have that same effect."

I whirled to see my dapper uncle, in his own long wool navy coat, dark bald head shining in the glow of the kitchen's light.

"How long have you been here?" I demanded.

"Long enough to know that we need to wake this sleeping giant all the way and get him out of here."

"What?" I asked. "Why? Doesn't he need to be here? In the North Pole? Getting all his minions back to work?"

"Sarah," Ah Lam said. "I thought you'd figured it out."

Now I was really confused. I looked from warlock to warlock, both of them groomed within an inch of their lives, both with studied, serious looks on their faces, as if I was a schoolchild who hadn't studied for the pop quiz.

What can I say? I'm a witch who goes by her instincts. I wear jeans and boots and only just keep my business afloat. I don't have access to the vast resources of the Council. And I don't want to. Well, not if it means I have to get all snooty and pay more for a pair of pants than I spend on clothing in a year.

"This isn't the North Pole," Cyrus finally said. "This is

an alternate realm where Old Nick is being held against his will."

"The sparkle?" I asked.

Ah Lam frowned. "I bet it is the vestiges of the spell that brought him here."

23

"How are we going to get him out of here?" I asked. "And what sort of dimension is this?"

I was familiar with in-between magical type places but had never been in one as fully realized as this. Having never been to Santa's village in the North Pole, I couldn't vouch for the accuracy of this place, but it sure as heck looked as I would have imagined it.

Before Cyrus or Ah Lam could answer, a commotion came from the hallway. Voices, the sound of boots, and a strange shushing sound.

All three of us squared our shoulders, ready for a fight. Santa just snorted again and mumbled something beneath his breath.

Jax's boots appeared first, then her wheelchair. Her dark eyes sparkled with fun, and a long purple scarf was wrapped around her neck, breaking up the rest of her black clothing. She was followed by Gabe, who wore a black anorak with a fake-fur lined hood. At least he'd finally traded out that leather jacket for something more sensible.

"We're in another alternate dimension!" Jax crowed. "Just like the one gran lives in!"

"This is so dope," Gabe agreed, looking around with interest.

When all of this was over, I really needed to sit down with these two plus Tracy and Tabitha and gather a bunch of notes on how this quantum physics stuff worked. I mean, as a witch, I had some vague passing knowledge of it, but still had not thought of it as real, if you know what I mean.

Which is odd, considering how many encounters I have with the shouldn't-be-real on a daily basis.

"Whoa," Jax said. "Is that an avatar of Santa?"

"That is the current embodied form of the old elf himself," Ah Lam replied."

"Wait," I said, "Santa is like an office, or a title, or something?"

"We have no time for this conversation," Cyrus said, tapping one Italian leather shoe in impatience. "The elf is about to awaken and we must get him safely contained before that happens."

Safely contained? When did Santa become a bomb?

"And how are we going to do that?" I asked, arms crossed over my chest. I wanted nothing more than to go home, take a shower, eat a tamale, and fall into bed to sleep for a solid eight to ten hours. But no, we had to deal with the latest Santa person without even a bracing cup of English Breakfast tea.

"Cyrus and I can pop everyone to the safe house."

"Or you can come with us into the worm hole!" Jax said, vibrating in her "chair.

"We don't know where the safe house is, remember?" Gabe said, leaning over to kiss Jax's forehead.

"Oh. Right."

I looked down at the Santa, who had moved again. His color really did look better. Less ghoul-like.

"It does look like he's waking up," I said. "All right. Let's do this."

"Cyrus, you take Sarah and Santa; I'll take care of these two. Who shouldn't be here in the first place." Ah Lam gave the two Goths a stern look. They both just beamed back at her, filled with excitement.

"Once we've transported the jolly old elf, we have got to have a team meeting," I insisted. "There are too many threads that need tying together, and I need everyone's focus on the problem."

Other than a couple of sharp nods, I got no response. I sighed, grabbed Cyrus's left hand as he placed his right around Santa's arm.

And then we whooshed out of not-the-North-Pole. My stomach lurched. I shut my eyes. Felt my feet land on a soft rug. Smelled frankincense and benzoin.

Opened my eyes to take in a long sectional sofa, sleek fireplace, and floor to ceiling plate glass looking out onto darkness and the shadows of trees.

We were in Uncle Cyrus's mid-century modern home in the swank hills on the west side of the Willamette river in Portland. It was his landing spot when he wasn't popping off to London, or Lagos, or New York. Portland was as close to Seashell Cove as he wished to live. It wasn't nearly large enough a city for his taste, but the Council had a mansion in Portland, and that, plus me, was enough for him to put up with a tree-filled burg of half a million people with enough cultural events to keep him mildly entertained.

The fact that he can pop to Paris anytime he wants helps.

"This is the safe house?" I asked, as he lay Santa out on the long side of the sofa.

"It's as safe as anyplace else," he replied. "And I just set up a new security system."

"You expect cameras and alarms to keep a magical being safe?" I crossed the lush geometric carpet to flop down on a wood and leather sling chair. Huh. It was pretty dang comfortable.

"No," he replied, heading to the fireplace to switch on the gas flames. "You have Petal and Posey, I have Rocky, Gypsum, and Slate."

I laughed. Of course, Cyrus had gargoyle guards.

"Gargoyles don't really match the mid-mod vibe you have going here."

He actually cracked a smile. "They remain well hidden. Most of the time."

Santa gave a mighty snort and rolled over.

"How long do you think he'll remain out of it? And shouldn't Ah Lam be here by now? And wait a minute, I thought my astral body was in that alternate dimension, but my physical body is here now. How the heck did that happen?"

I looked down at myself, feeling extra relieved that

urgent care didn't change people into hideous hospital gowns.

"And where's everyone else?"

Cyrus went very still, as if thinking. Or communicating with someone not here in the room. Probably the latter.

He blinked. "Ah Lam is en route. She dropped the others at your home. Everyone is waiting for you there."

My headache was back, and exhaustion was creeping up on me. Good thing I was sitting down.

"And how, exactly, am I supposed to get there? I don't have warlock powers! And shouldn't you two have figured this out before?"

Cyrus raised a placating hand. "No need to get grumpy with me."

"Who, exactly, am I supposed to be grumpy with?"

"With me," said a new voice. Both our heads snapped toward the couch, where the jolly old elf struggled to sit up on the couch, his red cardigan twisted around his rotund torso. He peered at me, then at Cyrus, then patted the patch pockets on his sweater, withdrawing a pair of round gold spectacles that he perched on a bulbous nose.

I hadn't gotten a good look at his face before, what with him being draped over a table and all. But yeah, he kinda looked like a classic Coca Cola Santa, but in more casual clothes.

"Why should I be grumpy with you?" I asked.

His green eyes focused on me. "Because I am the cause of your troubles."

There was a rumble and clatter outside and Cyrus snapped to attention, rushing to open one section of the floor to ceiling glass that turned out to be a huge sliding door.

Two fierce looking gargoyles perched on the shallow deck outside, trees whipping behind them.

"Boss," said one.

"We got trouble," said the second.

And that was a phrase a witch never wanted to hear. Guess this wasn't such a safe house after all.

Santa groaned and slowly stood.

"You are in no shape to be up," Cyrus protested.

Old Nick looked at my uncle. "Do we have a choice in the matter?"

"Boss!" The first gargoyle flapped its wings, stone screeching against stone in agitation.

I willed my headache away, found my center, called up my witch's power, and headed toward the open glass door.

24

The gargoyles made way for me. As soon as I stepped onto the deck, the wind whipped my hair around my face. I struggled to secure it with a random hair tie I pulled from my jeans.

Behind me, I heard Cyrus and Santa shove through the door. I stepped aside just in time to avoid being crushed by big elf boots. Santa looked haggard and determined. Was the guy ever jolly? Or was that just a marketing ploy?

I stifled the urge to shout, "I'll be good, for goodness' sake!" at his face. I really needed to keep myself together. That bonk on the head was making me weird.

Or weirder than usual.

Then, over the howling wind and the icy bite that presaged snow, I heard footsteps. And the shushing whir of a wheelchair. And the crackle of barely contained magic.

It seemed that, along with trouble, the cavalry had

arrived. I just hoped that, unlike cavalries of old, they didn't cause more damage than they staved off.

::We're in the driveway, headed toward the backyard!::

Rhiannon was here? How in the world...

::Stefon, too. Everyone is here.::

::How about Melchior?::

Rhiannon didn't answer, which meant...

"Duck!" I shouted, as a shimmering ball hurtled our way. Everyone on the shallow balcony lurched and dodged. The ball hit one of the gargoyle's wingtips, and I heard a crack.

"Gargoyle down!" the second gargoyle shouted. But there was no time to make sure Cyrus's sentry was okay.

"Stop that!" A voice called from down below. Was that Delta Crabbit? It sounded like the older witch, but with the wind and all, it was hard to tell. "I told you they are not the enemy!"

Oookaayy...

I leaned over the railing. "Delta! What the heck is going on down there?" And how did the crew get here so quickly? Cyrus's place was a two-hour drive from Seashell Cove.

"Come down and see!" That was Carol's voice. Everyone really was here. "But make it quick. Things are a bit...unruly."

::That's an understatement.::

"Told you there was a situation, boss," said one of the gargoyles as it swooped from the deck and up to the bare branches of one of the waiting dark trees.

"Stairs," Cyrus said. "Far end of the balcony."

Yeah, I never spent time here. Cyrus always came to

me. The only time I'd been here before was spent down in his daylight basement, watching over some frightened chaneques.

I rushed down the wood planks to the stairs hiding in the darkness at the end. Grateful for my boots, I thumped down and into Stefon's waiting arms.

"Oof!" The breath huffed out of me as my soft chest hit his much harder one. My sweetheart has a big gut, broad chest, and muscles for days. And I love every inch of him.

"How did you all get here?" I asked, peering around the back garden where solar lights cast soft puddles of gold around the covered swimming pool and planted rock cairns.

Jax wheeled toward me, followed by Delta, Carol, the teens, and Gabe.

"Ah Lam turned us into a human chain and ported us here!" Jax said. "It was amazing! Makes me want to take her to meet Gran."

Right. Jax's dead-but-not-dead grandmother who lived in some sort of alternate dimension. How in the nine worlds had my life gotten weirder than it already was?

"How's your head, babe?" Stefon asked, pulling me close.

I paused. Yep, still pounding, though not as badly as before.

"Still have a headache, but it seems to be getting better."

"Where's Santa?" Ah Lam finally appeared in the darkness, long wool coat brushing around her ankles as she walked toward us. She gave Cyrus a nod and he nodded back. I guess that was all they were allowed when actively working a case. I snuggled closer into Stefon's solid bulk. Another reason to not join the snooty Council. I was into PDA whenever I could get it.

Like, not gross, over the top PDA, but a light kiss or a cuddle? I'm all in.

"Upstairs. Why are you all here?"

"Because we need to have a meeting," Delta said. "Things are only getting worse and we still don't know the cause of all this mess!"

Delta sounded furious. Her body shook and there were angry tears in her eyes. She also seemed...scared.

I peeled away from Stefon. "Delta? What's wrong? Did something else happen?"

She let out a little sob just as Preston climbed out of the ubiquitous tote bag always slung over Delta's shoulder. Stefon stepped forward and offered the little gnome his arm. Preston clambered up until he was seated on my boyfriend's shoulder.

"It's the trees," Preston said, adjusting his red cap with the purple border. "They're getting worse."

"They're dying!" Delta snapped. "They're dying and I want to know who is at fault! Someone has put out a death warrant on them, and if it is that slumbering sham of a Nicholas upstairs..."

"Hey," Jax said, rolling her chair toward Delta. "It's probably not his fault. I dealt with a rogue Santa avatar once and it was...not pretty. Any manner of things could be wrong, and it might not be his fault."

I sighed. "Cyrus?"

We were standing in his backyard, and I really needed someone who didn't have a lump on their head to take charge for a little while. Even Justices need a break sometimes. That's why this Justice has a crew.

Cyrus clapped his hands. "All right. Everybody upstairs! Jax, there's a ramp out front."

Too weary to climb the stairs again, I followed my uncle up the incline of the side walkway leading back to the front. The thing about these hill-built houses is that you get great views and a proper walkout basement.

The other thing about houses in this neighborhood? They cost more than I could ever afford.

Soon enough, we were all gathered around the snoring Santa in Cyrus's living room. Guess he'd decided that being awake was too much effort. The gas fire was nice, but not as homey as my own wood-burning one. The teens and Carol commandeered the kitchen to make everyone tea.

Stefon had disappeared behind them and returned bearing a glass of water and a closed fist that I hoped held some pain reliever. It did.

"Thanks."

"No problem, love." He dropped a soft kiss on my head and sank into a chair next to me. Everyone was arrayed around the room in a variety of chairs or plopped on cushions. Maybe putting Santa on the couch was not the best idea.

"Should we be having this conversation in front of Santa?" I asked. "I mean, what if he's involved?"

::*Good point,*:: Rhiannon said.

::*Wait, are you here?*::

A furry black head poked itself out from Delta's tote bag, yawning as if she'd just awakened from a nap. The little black runt had stowed away with Preston!

::*Never call me a runt again.*::

Right. ::*My bad. I have a headache.*::

Rhiannon gave a soft growl but came to sit next to me anyway. She had to pretend to be offended, but it was nice to see she cared about me even so.

By the time we were done with our exchange, Gabe was helping Stefon to hoist a groggy and grumbling Santa off the couch with Cyrus's help. The three men were so unalike it was almost comical. Skinny Goth Gabe. My muscular, geeky knight of a boyfriend. And my too dapper for words honorary uncle. They somehow half dragged, half walked the barely coherent old elf toward the back hallway and to a guest room, I presumed.

"Ho, ho, ho," I heard Santa mumble down the hall.

Ho, ho, ho. I wished I was headed to bed myself.

25

A s a yawn threatened to crack my face in two, Tabitha, Tracy, and Carol emerged with steaming mugs of tea and a tray of milk, honey, sugar, and cookies.

I was frankly shocked that Cyrus kept anything so prosaic in what I was sure was a spotless kitchen. As far as I could tell, the man was strictly a fine wine and fine food kind of guy.

Delta took one end of the newly vacant sofa, and sat, arms crossed over her slight chest, chin down. Preston sat on the sofa arm next to her, occasionally patting her arm.

Carol and the teens took up the rest of the sofa.

"As soon as Cyrus returns, Delta is correct. We need to figure out a plan," Ah Lam said from a black sling chair near the big gas fire. "There is troubling magic afoot and the Council is not pleased."

"Pardon me," I said. "But the Council is the least of our worries right now."

"The Council," Cyrus said, taking the second chair

near the fire, "is of utmost concern. If they are not happy, it means the situation is very grave."

"I think we already figured that out," I muttered. Cyrus shot me a look, and Stefon gave me a pat on the thigh as he sat back down next to me. I wasn't sure if it was a warning to play nice, commiseration, or some combination of both.

Gabe slid bonelessly to a floor cushion next to Jax's wheelchair. "What's the Council?"

We all looked at him.

"Long story," Stefon finally said.

Gabe shrugged. "So, what's next?"

I doctored one of the mugs of tea with oat milk and a dash of sugar and settled back to think. I'd barely taken one sip when a ruckus sounded in the chimney.

"Turn off the gas!" Ah Lam shrieked. Cyrus leapt to his feet to turn a big metal key, dousing the flames, and not a moment too soon. A soot-stained little elf plopped its tiny butt onto the fake logs, followed by a whoosh of sparkling lights.

The Solstice Sprite had arrived.

"Ouch!" said Melchior, stumbling off the hearth and into Stefon's waiting hands.

"Gotcha!"

I hadn't even seen Stefon move, but his knightly reflexes must have kicked in at the first whiff of alarm. It's his own kind of magic, though he insists it's just years of training. Potay-to, potah-to.

The Solstice Sprite whooshed around the room a bit, in a dizzying array of festive sparkles that should have been entertaining but...wasn't. The sprite finally perched on Jax's knee and began preening soot from her sparkling wings.

Melchior pulled a handkerchief from one tiny pocket and scrubbed at his pale green face.

"Is that tea?" he asked, voice plaintive. "Or do you have hot chocolate?"

"I'll get you a cup," Tracy said, leaping from the sofa. She returned seconds later with an espresso cup of tea that still looked too large for Melchior's hands.

"Sorry," Tracy said. "No hot chocolate, but there's a lot of sugar in there."

Melchior nodded his thanks and drank deeply, smacking his lips in pleasure.

"Melchior," I said, once the little elf seemed calm. "What happened? Are you all right?"

"Sprite said we had to get out of town," he said.

Ah Lam leaned forward. "Where did you go?"

"To some fancy mansion not far from here. It was filled with ghosts."

That was the mansion where the Council held its local meetings. It was also the place where we'd almost lost Cyrus. It also seemed like an odd place for a Solstice Sprite to end up. Ah Lam and Cyrus seemed to think so, too, given the look they exchanged.

"But we didn't stay there long. She took me all sorts of places. Like the tree farm. And a place that really wasn't the North Pole. We also visited a place that looked like spring, and another that felt like summer."

He slurped some more tea, then set the cup on the coffee table. "But that wasn't the weird part."

This time, we all leaned forward.

"The weird part is, everywhere we went, the two brothers were there. And they were fighting."

"Oh, no," Tabitha groaned. "That is very, very bad."

"What do you mean?" Jax asked, as we all turned to face the Tabitha.

She shook her wedge of straight black hair, the purple streak swinging, then fingered the silver pentacle at her throat.

"Tabitha?" Ah Lam asked. The young Goth Wiccan raised her eyes to the warlock. Again, with the silent communication. But this time, I wondered if Cyrus and I shouldn't rope Ah Lam into the teen's training regimen. It might do Tabitha good to have a person of Asian descent to help her navigate some of the social aspects of our interlocking magical worlds. Our parts of Oregon might think they're progressive, but racism is still a big deal here. Stefon and my ex, Cecilia, remind me of that all the time.

"The Oak King and the Holly King are supposed to trade off, and they know that. Their fight is only supposed to signal how long winter or summer will last. If the fight becomes eternal..."

"If the fight becomes eternal, then we end up in eternal winter or summer or some terrible combination of the two," Jax whispered. "The seas will rise, the ice will melt, the sun will grow hotter, the storms more severe."

"Sounds like climate change," Stefon said.

Exactly. Which meant ordinary human activity was

affecting the mythological and magical worlds. And that meant very, very big trouble. Bigger trouble than our little crew had ever faced before.

"No wonder the Council is upset," I said.

"Indeed," Cyrus replied, crossing his legs and steepling his fingers at his chin.

"How many Holly and Oak Kings are there?" I asked. "I mean, those two seemed friendly enough in Seashell Cove."

"They are also trapped in some sideways realms," a new voice said. It was Santa, looking exhausted, leaning against the door jamb leading to the hallway, fists stuffed in the pockets of his red cardigan. "Some force beyond our control is making multiverses and trapping aspects of all the seasonal avatars there. Some have been able to escape, but most..."

"Most are repeating their actions, over and over again," Gabe interjected. "Just like Jax's grandmother predicted. Someone with knowledge of quantum physics and magic has used that to gain control."

"But to what end?" Stefon asked.

And wasn't that the question of the hour?

26

My eyes were gritty with exhaustion, and I yawned over my first cup of English Breakfast tea, leaning heavily on the bookshop counter and going over yesterday's books. Rhiannon was perched on the edge of the counter, doing her morning ablutions. I took a fortifying sip and addressed the numbers.

Our ragtag group of magical investigators had talked long into the night and gotten nowhere. I still had no clues as to who was stealing magical beings away and secreting them in various worlds, including my shop. Which reminded me...

"How are you doing, Melchior?"

"Sleepy." The elf's voice was barely audible and came from high on a bookshelf near the center of the shop.

"Thank the Stone Gods," Petal muttered. I owed both Petal and Posey nice gifts for all their work corralling the little elf. Would gargoyles like winter scarves? Did they even get cold?

I returned my attention to the books. The shop had done well in my brief absence, thanks to Duncan and the teens. But haring off to get my head conked by a rock was not the best plan during the rush leading up to Yule. Luckily, my concussion had been pronounced mild.

Though "mild concussion" might account for the complete bonkers nature of everything that followed.

But thinking of Yule reminded me, I still hadn't found the right present for Stefon. I knew what I wanted to give him, but the thought of it made my hands break out in a sweat.

::*Scaredy cat*.:: Rhiannon paused in washing her paw to glare at me with those inscrutable amber eyes.

"As if you've ever been in love and needed to have another discussion with your partner about possible cohabitation."

Like, I know we both wanted to, but who was going to give up their home and move? And would we still be in love if we saw each other's weird habits on the daily?

::*You humans are funny*,:: she replied, but thankfully said no more.

Thing is, the cat wasn't wrong. We humans are funny about love and relationships, even people like Stefon and I, who had both had plenty of lovers of all genders and descriptions. Well. "Plenty" was an overstatement, but neither of us was inexperienced. We'd both slid into an unspoken monogamy despite having been firmly anarchistic in our relationships before. Even when Cecilia and I were together, we dated other people on occasion.

I would blame the slide into social normalcy on aging, but mostly it was just that we were both so busy.

And besides, Stefon had just become my person, much as I loved my friends.

It was surprisingly slow for a pre-holiday morning, but I was grateful for the respite. Duncan would be in later, along with Tracy and Tabitha, but it was nice to have The Widening Gyre to myself for a bit. I hadn't even turned music on, so the only sounds were the gargoyles shifting themselves on the bookcases and the soft rasp of Rhiannon's tongue. Even the cars outside were muffled by the glass in the display windows.

Looking past the fairy lights that framed the big windows, I frowned. The clouds were the sort of black that threatened snow. Snow on the coast was no joke, considering we didn't have the infrastructure to deal with anything more than the lightest dusting.

As I gazed out the window, mug warming my hands, the bell on the front door chimed.

In trotted the unicorn, with the monarch lady on its back. I shivered to look at her. How she could be out in the cold air wearing nothing but an artfully draped piece of gauze was beyond me. Though, considering she'd been stark naked before, maybe the gauze was considered protection enough against the wintery elements? My shoulders hunched a bit in my cranberry wool sweater, as if I could ward off the cold outside.

The unicorn stopped a few feet from the counter and the monarch lady drew herself up to her full, tiny height, and raised her chin as if she could look down on me.

"I have come for the elf," she declared. And she really did declare it, like, I'm not just using a fancy word for *said* here.

"I haven't seen the elf," I replied. Which was technically true. I had only heard Melchior.

A sound like rocks falling down a hill sounded from the rear of the store. One of the gargoyles, laughing. Great. Just what I needed. Something to draw the persnickety monarch lady's attention toward Melchior's hiding place.

Luckily, she didn't seem to notice, fixating instead at Rhiannon, who was having some sort of inter-species staring contest with the monarch. The little unicorn was craning its long white neck in the opposite direction though, as if it could see through the bookcases all the way in the back.

Which meant I needed to keep an eye on it.

"Have you ascertained what is disrupting the realms?" the monarch lady asked, arching one tiny brow.

::It's her,:: Rhiannon thought my way.

::What?::

::Causing the disturbances. It's her.::

"Why do you not answer me?" If she hadn't been unicorn-back, she would've stamped one of her little perfectly formed feet.

"I'm thinking," I replied quickly. "We've been doing our best to gather information, but the short answer is no."

Switching back to the mind speech channel Rhiannon had opened, I thought back, *::How can you tell?::*

::She has silvery sparkles on her head. Like she's been somewhere with snow.::

I looked back at the monarch and Rhiannon was

right, tiny glimmers of silver and white sparkled on her hair. My eyes must have narrowed, because the monarch lady reached up and ran a pale orange hand over her dark head of hair.

"It's cold out," she said, staring as if daring me to contradict her.

"It sure is. I'm surprised you don't need warmer clothing."

She shrugged her tiny, sharp shoulders. "I carry summer with me, wherever I go."

"Tell me," I asked, pretending to straighten some of the displays on the counter. "How did you end up here, again?"

"I told you! We were kidnapped. Brought to this realm against our will!"

::*As if,*:: Rhiannon muttered. The tip of her tail twitched.

I heard a soft scraping sound. The gargoyles must be moving.

"It just seems odd to me," I replied, "that an elf shows up on my doorstep, announcing that 'he is coming' but 'he' is trapped in some alternate world and not going anywhere. And then you show up immediately after. What do you say to that?"

Her face screwed up in anger. Then, quicker than I could blink, the monarch lady flung a magic bolt at my head.

I barely ducked in time.

27

Lily the unicorn charged, driving his horn into the front counter with a splintering crash. I was really glad the thing wasn't full sized.

"Around the counter, you fool!" the monarch lady shouted.

Oh no. No way was I getting trapped back here with a berserker avatar of summer. Especially an avatar of summer who seemed intent on doing me harm.

I rushed around the counter just as Rhiannon leapt on the unicorn's white rump. The creature squealed in pain, trying to buck Rhiannon off as the monarch clung to its mane.

Its horn was still embedded in the wood of the front counter.

::Thanks, cat!::

The door burst open, bells clattering, and Stefon— with Preston the gnome riding one shoulder—Carol, Tabitha, and Tracy rushed in, followed by Delta Crabbit.

The gargoyles swooped overhead, almost dashing

Cyrus in his bald head as he and Ah Lam Wu rounded the bookcases from the back. A book flew through the air, barely missing the unicorn's horn. Wow. That meant Biff was in on the action, too.

Stefon grabbed me. "You okay?"

"Fine!" I nodded. "How are you all here?"

He shrugged, then ducked as a bolt of orange sparkly fire passed between us. Dang monarch lady had good aim, even on a bucking mini-unicorn.

"Rhiannon called Preston or something? I don't know how this stuff works."

Two more sparkly bolts zinged past.

"Got anything to block this?" Stefon growled as I countered with a blast of magic of my own. I wished he wasn't here. He might be a part-time knight, but had zero actual magic.

"Grab the sign behind the counter!"

We had a wooden sandwich board for the front sidewalk. Luckily, I hadn't put it out for the day yet.

The unicorn got itself unstuck and kicked one more time, hard. Rhiannon and the monarch lady went flying, Rhiannon's yowls splitting the air like a chainsaw cutting logs. The monarch flapped furiously, only to be backhanded by a flying Petal, stone bow firmly affixed to her stone head. The monarch cartwheeled toward Ah Lam, who held out her hands.

She was backed up by Cyrus, and together, they formed a sort of force field that trapped the monarch, who fluttered and beat at the edges of the energetic container.

"This is only temporary!" Ah Lam shouted. I could

already see perspiration dotting her otherwise perfectly smooth brow.

"What's the plan?" Tabitha asked. Both teens were near the front door, as if to block the entrance. The entrance of what, though?

I thought quickly. Preston was stuck to the unicorn's back like a bull rider, as Rhiannon wound her way near the white creature's sharp-looking hooves.

A pounding started on the door.

"It's Mr. Vargas!" Tracy squealed, opening the door.

"Stefon?" I asked, turning behind me.

He looked startled, half-raised wooden sandwich board still gripped in his hands. "Uh. Yeah?"

"Can you help Preston and Rhiannon?"

"What do you want me to do?" He looked at the bucking, stumbling mini-unicorn with skepticism.

The pounding on the door increased, but I had to make sure the unicorn didn't make a run for it.

"I don't know! Sit on it or something!"

Stefon grabbed the unicorn's neck from behind. It turned its head, trying to bite. Tabitha rushed forward and wrapped her scarf around the unicorn's neck. I trusted the two of them to tether the thing. For now.

"Let Mr. Vargas in."

Tracy nodded and opened the door. Carol and Delta whispered near one of the bookcases. I hoped they were coming up with something useful, because I sure as heck wasn't.

Mr. Vargas rushed in, followed by the scent of coming snow. His arms were outstretched and filled with with spruce branches.

"Delta! The trees! They need your magic, now!"

Delta fell to her knees, a sob wrenching her throat. She held out her own arms and he filled them with the fragrant branches.

"We need a plan!" Ah Lam said again, her voice strained.

"Hurry, Sarah!" Cyrus added.

Then the pounding at the door began again. Books flew through the air and thumped all over the floor. There was too much noise. Too much confusion for my recently injured head. I held my hands to my temples and tried to slow my breathing down.

"Delta! You and Mr. Vargas do what you need to for the trees." They both nodded and headed for the door.

"Tabitha! Can you hold the unicorn? Tracy, see who is at the door. Carol and Stefon, get ready to back her up. Petal and Posey, guard the store!"

I didn't want to tell them who to guard, not out loud, but figured the gargoyles knew I meant Melchior.

"And Biff...stop throwing things until someone tells you to."

There. I'd bought myself thirty seconds, and that was all I needed.

I hoped.

I slowed my breathing down and dropped into my center, feeling my feet connect with the earth beneath the foundation of the store, and feeling sky, ocean, clouds, and my friends around me. I tasted the power of the salty, snowy air. I drew on all of it.

I drew up power from the earth. Power from the gathering storm and the ocean. Power from the love and magic of the friends surrounding me.

Then I called upon the power of the office of Justice. Felt it fill me, warm and golden, slipping through my bloodstream, through my body, before spilling out into the energy fields that traced the edges of my skin.

I raised my hands just as Stefon opened the door, Carol raised her hands, ready to do some defensive magic, and the Oak and Holly King burst through, followed by Santa.

Great. More chaos had arrived.

"Be. Still!" I put every lick of power into my words and held up my hands in the universal symbol of Stop.

And everything did. Stop, I mean.

I'd need to apologize to my friends later for non-consensually freezing them like that, but the Justice in me had to slow things down. All the way down.

Finally, it was quiet enough in the store for me to think. I exhaled, then cast out my witchy senses once again, seeking information, seeking a way out of this mess....

A thought tickled at the base of my skull. I knew what needed to happen.

I just hoped we weren't too late.

"Everyone, we're going to the tree farm. Together. Keep the unicorn and the monarch contained. And someone call Jax and Gabe and have them meet us there."

No one moved. Right.

"I'm going to unfreeze you all in thirteen seconds.

Make sure the monarch lady and the unicorn don't get free."

My inner clocked ticked down. I could feel my friends preparing to move. Unfortunately, I could feel the monarch and unicorn doing the same. And the jury was still out on the warring brothers and our sleepy Santa.

"Now!" I shouted, releasing the magic.

Cyrus threw a silk scarf over the monarch lady, temporarily blinding her, as Ah Lam wound the rest of the scarf around her wings and body, swaddling her in an insulating layer. Good idea. Silk dampened magic.

Tabitha jerked on the scarf around the unicorn's neck as its hooves scrabbled on the wood floor. I was going to need to buff the scrapes out later.

"I'm out of here. You're on your own, you tyrant!" the unicorn said, and winked out of existence.

I heard the monarch lady shriek inside her silk wrappings. Huh. No honor among rogue magical beings, I guess. Or the unicorn just got tired of being in her thrall. I didn't blame the thing.

"What now?" Tabitha asked, scarf dangling from her hands.

"I'm going to get my coat. Then we have to figure out how to carpool to Delta's farm. We have to save those trees."

28

I clutched my belly, really wishing we'd carpooled as I'd suggested, but no, Ah Lam Wu had said we didn't have time. Gah. I really hated teleportation. And my post-mild-concussion head *really* didn't appreciate it.

Beside me, Stefon groaned.

"How do you handle that?" he asked, staggering into the Yule Tree parking lot when our feet touched ground.

"I don't," I replied, taking slow deep breaths of the frigid air. The popping in and out sensation was the pits. If I ever wanted to lose weight—which I don't, thank you very much—I'd just have Cyrus teleport me hither and yon. I'd never want to eat again.

Warlocks must either be born acclimated or have acquired immunity after years of training. Ah Lam and Uncle Cyrus both looked sleek and unruffled as always. The monarch lady was limp in her swaddling, tucked inside my coat. Good. Maybe she was asleep and would stay that way.

If we were lucky.

Everyone else looked a bit green around the gills as well, but we didn't have time to rest. The air already hummed with magic. And not magic I recognized.

Great. That meant the monarch lady wasn't our only problem. Mr. Vargas rushed toward us.

"Come! Quickly! Delta needs you!"

We all burst into a trot, except for Jax, who muscled the wheels of her 'chair as if she was training for the Paralympics. Impressive.

The magic humming was coming from the sickly trees. Well, not from them. Around them. Delta stood at the base of the center tree, hat off, short gray hair wild. Her hands were raised, and she traced symbols in the frosty air. Preston stood next to her in the light dusting of snow. His own arms were held straight out. I wasn't sure if he was pointing at something, engaged in a summoning, or holding something at bay.

Note to self: learn more about gnomish magic.

Above our heads, something glittery was winking in and out, as if weaving around the sickly trees.

"Is that the Solstice Sprite?" Tabitha asked. "I've always wanted to see one."

The Solstice Sprite. The sprite that caused my concussion. The sprite that put Melchior in danger. The Solstice Sprite was in the trees! That could only be bad....

I reached past the lurching feeling in my stomach for a glimmering of my Justice's power and gathered as much as I could, then threw it into my voice.

"Get away from those trees!" I shouted. The shimmering swerved and dived, careening toward the ground before the sprite caught herself and flew steadily toward us.

The sprite shrieked and chittered in my face. Which was mildly terrifying. I stood my ground.

"So we see," Cyrus's voice was deadly calm, which meant he was angry. And that he could understand what the angry sprite was saying.

"What are you doing to the trees?" I shouted.

"Sarah!" Delta's voice cracked through the air. "The sprite was helping me. Helping me..."

Then the older witch's voice broke, and she crumpled toward the ground. Preston barely jumped out of the way in time. Tracy and Tabitha rushed to help her, followed by Carol. Jax and Gabe were doing something or other, heads tilted close.

Mr. Vargas was wringing his hands in distress.

Then something kicked me, hard, in the stomach.

"Ouch!"

"Uh, babe, your coat is squirming," Stefon said.

Dang! I unzipped the top of my coat and looked down, craning my neck to see past my chest. An angry monarch lady glared back at me.

"How dare you hold me captive?" she shrieked.

The Solstice Sprite shouted what sounded like a string of curse words, then dove into the opening of my coat.

"No! No way are you fighting in my... No! Gah!" But they were. And wow was that painful! Who knew that such tiny creatures could kick and punch so hard?

"Stefon!" I gasped. "Help!"

He grabbed my zipper, yanked down hard, and the

sprite and monarch tumbled to the snow, still grappling, the scarf that had been wrapped around the monarch tangling them both now. It looked as if summer and winter were duking it out as the snow began to fall again.

What in the world was going on?

::*Throw some water on them!*:: Rhiannon shouted in my head.

I turned to see the black cat mincing her way across the snow. Who in the world had she ridden here with?

"I don't have any water!" But I sure as heck didn't want to reach into the fray to try and separate the two.

"I'll get 'em, babe," said Stefon. Pulling a thick pair of gloves from his jacket, he slid them on, face grim.

Then he reached in, grabbed the sprite in one hand and the monarch in the other, and lifted the still punching and kicking bodies into the air.

"Now what?" he asked.

"We'll take them." The Oak King was here, his brother at his side. When the heck had they arrived? Delta's tree farm was becoming Grand Central Station for magical and legendary beings.

"Uh, I don't think so," Stefon said, clutching his charges. "I don't exactly know if we can trust you two."

The Holly King exhaled, breath a white plume in the air.

"We are quite trustworthy!" the Oak King blustered. He really was looking a bit worse for the wear.

"I don't know about that," I replied, looking from one brother to the next, eyes fixing on the Holly King's. "You were in the shop the day Melchior and the Solstice Sprite first appeared, and considering this is your season, you seem to have a vested interest in all of this."

"Why would I want Santa swept into an alternate dimension? Yule is my season! I am Lord of the Solstice-tide! Santa is part of that, as is the Solstice Sprite."

"I'll vouch for him," Santa said. "For both of them. The Sacred Brothers would not wish harm upon me or any of my people."

I heard a tiny sob and Melchior rushed forth to clutch at Santa's leg. The little elf looked up at me. "I told you he was coming!"

Wait. "You were talking about Santa? And does this mean you remember?"

"Of course," Santa replied. "Melchior is my herald. When I went missing, he must have gone missing, too."

Melchior gazed adoringly at Santa. "I remember now, I do!"

If the Brothers, Santa, and the Solstice Sprite were innocent—though given the bump on my head, the latter was still slightly suspect—that only left one being.

"Melchior, do you remember what happened right before your memory left and you ended up in my bookshop?"

The wee elf nodded. "The monarch lady said she wanted a gift for a friend. I was writing down her order like I'm supposed to, but then...everything went away."

Great. The monarch lady hadn't been kidnapped. She'd fooled everyone. Which didn't make me feel any better about being duped.

"Your Graceful Flight," I said. "Why have you done these things?"

The little monarch sniffed. "Because Summer is just as necessary as Winter! But we don't get special celebrations that last for months at a time, now do we? It's all The Winter Holidays this and that, all the time!"

All the humans looked at each other and began to laugh.

"What?" If the monarch lady had been on the ground, she would have stomped one of her little feet.

"This is Seashell Cove," Tracy replied. "People who live here do nothing but celebrate summer! It is the time of year when our town is filled!"

"But there aren't lights. And presents. And candles. And gifts..."

Tabitha stepped forward. "There are kites flying, and children laughing, and ice cream, and taffy, and swimming. There are picnics and races and music. Summer is what keeps Seashell Cove alive."

"Are you trying to trick me?" The monarch lady asked.

"They're not," Preston said. "What the young women say is true. I have seen it, time and time again."

"Are you going to punish me?" the monarch lady asked.

Everyone turned to look at me. Right. Every person here might be responsible for keeping the scales of justice balanced here in Seashell Cove, but I was the final word.

"Yes. Lucky for you the trees aren't dead yet, or you'd have a murder charge on your hands. As it is, you have kidnapped people, and lied, and formed alternate universes that should not exist."

"But…"

I held up a hand to forestall whatever protestations were coming. I'd pretty much had enough of Her Graceful Flight. As far as I was concerned, I wanted her to fly as far away from Seashell Cove as possible. But banishing was not nearly recompense enough.

I pulled up the power of Justice to make my words binding.

"Your Graceful Flight, I charge you with malicious interference and attempted murder. You must be held accountable for your actions. I charge you to help set things to rights. You must work with Jax, Gabe, and the warlocks on shutting down the alternate universes you helped to create. But first…"

I gazed up at the towering, sickly spruces.

"You will help us fix these trees."

29

We all gathered around, ringing the three towering spruces that represented the health, vitality, and magic of the Yule Tree Farm and the surrounding land.

Mr. Vargas and Delta stood in the center of the circle, closest to the trees. I couldn't quite see the people on the other side but felt them there. All of us, old friends and new, legends and antagonists, magical beings and ordinary human beings. Witches, warlocks, gnomes, sprites, and seasonal avatars.

I slowed my breathing down and felt the snowy ground beneath my feet. I tasted the cold and magic on the air. Mint and chocolate and sweet oranges. Woodsmoke and balsam.

"Breathe it in," I said, pitching my voice to carry. "Breathe in the goodness of this season and draw upon the strength of this land. Feel every part of you that feels a longing for magic. Feel every part of you that feels lost or lonely, unappreciated or unseen. Feel the parts of you that are healthy and the parts that need healing still."

We were all silent then, with only the breeze through the trees, the soft fall of snow, and a faint chiming of bells.

"Now connect that magic—the magic of this place and the magic inside you—with each other. Hold out your hands and connect with the people around you."

Stefon's gloved hand slid around mine, and Carol grabbed my other hand. Hand to hand, the magic passed, until the circle was complete. I felt a snap up my spine, then a slight tingling that meant our circle was complete.

"Tabitha?" I looked across at the young Goth Wiccan with her gorgeous Asian features and the pink pentagram on her black watch cap. She nodded.

"Take this circle," she began, "and imagine pushing it up and down, forming arcs above and below us, until our magic forms a mighty sphere. Connect your sense of love and friendship, your sense of gratitude of all of us here, in this place and time."

And everyone did. On three great breaths, the sphere rose above and pushed beneath us.

"Delta? Mr. Vargas?"

The two figures in the center of sphere both nodded, then began circling the trees, weaving in and out among the three giants, patting their bark with their hands, leaning in to whisper to the low-hanging branches.

"Feed the power to those two and those three!" I called out. "Hold your hands toward the center and lend them your strength!"

We all did. I could see multicolored strands of magic

weaving and pulsating toward Delta, Mr. Vargas, and the trees.

Someone started a low humming that rose and fell. Stefon began to stomp one booted foot onto the ground, pounding out a rhythm. The humming resolved into a chant. First the Holly King, then the Oak. Then, one by one, other voices joined in, rising in harmony.

"We call upon the sleeping sap, we call upon the slumbering sun. We call the quiet earth and ocean storms. We call upon those gathered here, to sing and dance and heal as one," the Holly King sang.

"We call upon the sacred gates that twine between the stars. We call the holy powers three, and nine, and twelve, and none." the Oak King continued.

"We call upon the shortest day," Tracy chimed in.

"We call upon the longest night," sang Tabitha.

"We call on the healing tides," Cyrus's lower voice joined in.

"We call on you with all our might!" everyone sang, voices growing louder.

Something was happening with the trees. The Solstice Sprite and monarch both flew into the air, weaving winter white and summer orange sparkles around the drooping branches. The trees shook and shimmered as if stirred by winds coming from every direction.

On and on we sang, with more and more of us stamping our boots and clapping our hands now.

"We call upon the shortest day! We call upon the longest night! We call upon the healing tides! We call on you with all our might!"

Delta and Mr. Vargas crouched toward the snowy ground, then raised their arms as high as they could, as if drawing power from the slumbering earth up toward the top peaks of the spruce trees. Over and over, they motioned down to up, up to down, with the winged monarch and sprite weaving magic side to side, forming a glowing tapestry of health and healing.

The trees began to plump up. Needles that had fallen to the earth rose once again, attaching themselves to bare limbs. Green shoots pushed from the tips, out of season, almost glowing amid the gently falling snow.

Our voices resolved to wordless chanting as the power built, and we began to circle the trees, stepping, stomping, or wheeling our way in a sunwise arc, pushing the tides toward what was yet to come.

Tears rolled down my cheeks as the power grew. Cold, hidden spaces within my heart and soul were filled again with warmth and light. I felt my mother and my father with me. I felt the whole lineage of witches whose lives had brought mine here, to this place.

In the center of our dancing circle, the trees lifted their limbs and swayed. All around us I felt the forest awaken to our song.

The song of the multiverses. The song of the nine worlds and those beyond. The song of magic. The song of life.

It was glorious. Beautiful.

There was a rightness restored to the world. A rightness in my soul and the soul of this land. A rightness from the North Pole to the South, from the longest night to the shortest.

It was the purest form of justice I had ever felt.

I breathed it in, expanding my heart to take it in.

And then...our voices quieted, falling off one by one; our feet stopped stomping and our clapping hands were still.

In midair, the monarch lady and the Solstice Sprite bowed to one another, then the Solstice Sprite winked out of sight. The monarch lady fluttered down to the snowy ground near my boots. She looked haggard, as if she had expended more magic than she had hoped.

Good.

Balance was restored, for the moment at least.

Then Jax wheeled her chair toward me, followed by Gabe, Cyrus, and Ah Lam.

"We'll finish the rest," Jax said. "We'll make sure the alternate realities are properly shut down. Climb aboard, Your Graceful Flight."

30

After the alternate realities were properly shut down, Cyrus and Ah Lam escorted Santa and Melchior back to the North Pole. The real North Pole, not the weird, in-between world I had visited. The Oak and Holly King went on their ways.

It was hard to believe that all the strange things that had happened were because the monarch lady felt slighted. I was glad that more harm hadn't been done, and hoped she felt reassured that the Summer Solstice was as important as Winter Solstice.

I also hoped I never had to see her again.

Speaking of seasonal celebrations, it was the longest night—Solstice Eve—and everyone had gathered in my overcrowded living room for a small Yule celebration. The fire was lit and one of Loreena McKennitt's winter albums played softly on Dad's old CD player.

Jax and Gabe were still in town, which pleased me, and were talking with Cecilia and Toby the hob near the fire. Tracy, Tabitha, and Carol were setting out treats in the kitchen. I'm not sure what I would do without those three.

Delta Crabbit had brought me a small tree, which she and Stefon had set up in the corner of the room near a bookcase. Preston was helping them decorate, and Rhiannon was, too. If you can call batting ornaments around with her paws helpful.

Me? I sat on the sofa, staring at the crackling fire, a mug of warm cider in my hands. I felt content.

This was my life: surrounded by friends and magic, with a partner who loved me and a store that brought people together and kept me and Rhiannon in food.

Finally, Carol and the teens brought out a tray filled with more mugs of cider.

"There are cookies and savory snacks in the kitchen, but we thought it might be nice to make a toast!" Tabitha said, grinning ear to ear.

Delta accepted a mug, then cleared her throat.

"I'd like to say something, first," the older witch said.

We all waited.

"I want to thank you all for helping the trees, and for helping me. Not so long ago, I thought I was alone in the world, but all of you have helped me see that isn't so. So, Happy Solstice, and Merry Yule!"

She raised her mug. We raised ours, too.

"Happy Solstice and Merry Yule!"

Delta looked at me. "Sarah?"

I smiled at all the beaming faces around the room.

"Stefon, would you turn off the music?" He complied, and a hush fell over the room. The fire spit and crackled. The cider in my mug was warm.

"On this longest night, I pray to all the Gods and Goddesses who are listening: may every person have warmth. May every person have food, shelter, and drink. May all beings know their place in the world. May all beings be well."

We all toasted once again, and then Tracy began to sing:

"We wait in the dark for the light to appear, Mother, give birth to our brother the sun!"

The chant wove around the room.

"We wait, we watch, out of the cold comes the promise of newness, out of the dark comes the promise of day!"

That's it, I thought. Day and night, dark and light... every moment is filled with promise, if we let it be so. Every moment is a chance.

The longest night heralds the coming day.

"Merry Yule!" I said, once the chanting was over. "Let us eat, drink, and be merry!"

And we did.

If you enjoy this series, you may also want to check out Thorn's other cozy paranormal series: Pride Street!

A waiter at the neighborhood sushi joint drops dead and gossip flies. Can cute corgis Marsha and Klaus sniff out what happened before the killer strikes again?

Find out what happens in **Sushi Scandal**, *available at your favorite bookseller or direct from the author!*

SUSHI
SCANDAL
A Pride Street
Paranormal Cozy Mystery
T. THORN COYLE
author of The Jeweled Cave Paranormal Mysteries

AND MORE...

If you enjoyed this book, please consider telling a friend, or leaving a short review at your favorite booksellers. Many thanks!

And visit thorncoyle.com to sign up for a weekly newsletter and for announcements on future dispatches from Rhiannon, Sarah, and their friends. Buy ebooks direct at thorncoylebooks.com

ACKNOWLEDGMENTS

Thank you to Leslie and Jack for reading, to Dayle for editing, and to my chosen family for years of support.

Most of all, thank you to everyone who fell in love with a witch, a cat, and a wacky seaside town.

ALSO BY T. THORN COYLE

FICTION

Seashell Cove Paranormal Cozy Mysteries

Bookshop Witch

Haunted Witch

Tarot Witch

Running Witch

Hallows Witch

Solstice Witch

The Pride Street Paranormal Cozy Mysteries

Sushi Scandal

Flower Frenzy

Muffin Murder

Hairspray Horror

The Mouse Thief

Mouse's Folly

Mouse's Fight

The Witches of Portland (complete)

By Earth

By Flame

By Wind

By Sea

By Moon

By Sun

By Dusk

By Dark

By Witch's Mark

The Panther Chronicles (Complete)

To Raise a Clenched Fist to the Sky

To Wrest Our Bodies From the Fire

To Drown This Fury in the Sea

To Stand With Power on This Ground

The Steel Clan Saga

We Seek No Kings

We Heed No Laws

We Ride at Night

Short Story Collections

A Hint of Faery

A Touch of Faery

A Spark of Magic

A Flame for Yuletide

A Hope for Winter

A Time for Magic

A Speculation of Stars

A Speculation of Hope

A Speculation of Time

Risk It All: Queer Stories of Love, Suspense, And Daring

Thresholds: Queer Stories of Love, Suspense, And Daring

Ghost Talker

Cats and Other Creatures

NON-FICTION

You are the Spell (late 2024)

Sigil Magic for Writers, Artists, & Other Creatives

Crafting a Daily Practice

Resistance Matters

Evolutionary Witchcraft

Kissing the Limitless

Make Magic of Your Life

ABOUT THE AUTHOR

T. Thorn Coyle worked in many strange and diverse occupations before settling in to write books full time.

Author of the *Seashell Cove Paranormal Mystery* series, the *Pride Street Paranormal Cozy Mysteries*, *The Steel Clan Saga*, *The Witches of Portland*, and *The Panther Chronicles*, Thorn's multiple non-fiction books include *Sigil Magic for Writers, Artists & Other Creatives*, *Kissing the Limitless*, *Make Magic of Your Life*, and *Evolutionary Witchcraft*. Thorn's work also appears in many anthologies, magazines, and collections.

An interloper to the Pacific Northwest U.S., Thorn drinks a lot of tea, pays proper tribute to the neighborhood cats, and talks to crows, squirrels, and trees.

Connect with Thorn:
www.thorncoyle.com